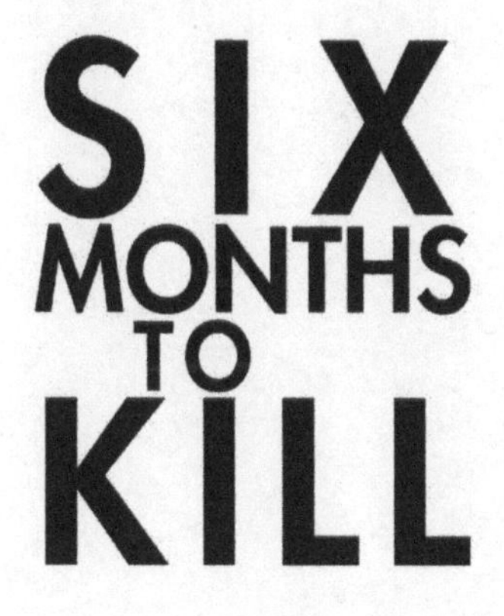
SIX
MONTHS
TO
KILL

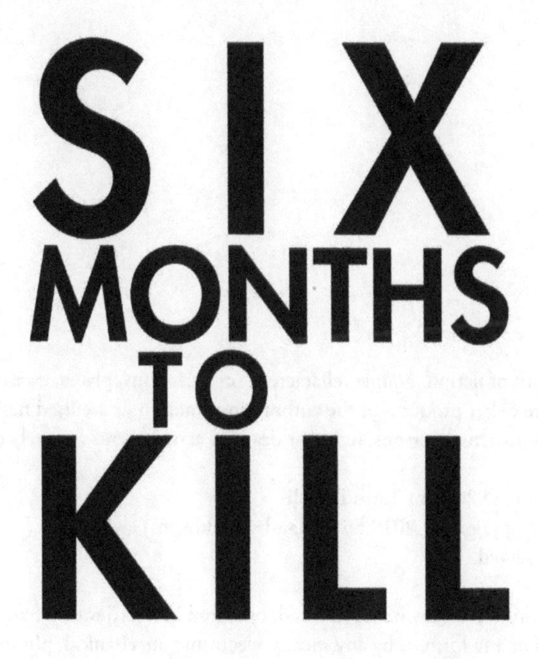
SIX
MONTHS
TO
KILL

ENZO BARTOLI
Translated by ALEXANDRA MALDWYN-DAVIES

THOMAS & MERCER

This is a work of fiction. Names, characters, organizations, places, events, and incidents are either products of the author's imagination or are used fictitiously. Any resemblance to actual persons, living or dead, or actual events is purely coincidental.

Previously published as *Six Mois à Tuer* by Thomas & Mercer in Luxembourg in 2017. Translated from French by Alexandra Maldwyn-Davies. First published in English by Thomas & Mercer in collaboration with Amazon Crossing in 2019.

Published by Thomas & Mercer, in collaboration with Amazon Crossing, Seattle

www.apub.com

ISBN-13: 9781542093767
ISBN-10: 1542093767

Cover design by kid-ethic

Printed in the United States of America

First edition

SIX
MONTHS
TO
KILL

Prologue

'Monsieur Gaudin, you're going to have to be brave about this,' declares Professor Lazreg, unable to hide a hint of sadness in his voice.

This eminent oncologist, who has been treating me for a good few months now, explains with calm deliberation that the cancer cells are growing at a much faster rate than anticipated and that the various treatments I've been subjected to haven't yielded the desired results. He avoids sentimentality, which is fine by me, and adds that any other therapies would only serve to make my final days increasingly distressing, and that there'd be no guarantee in terms of delaying the inevitable.

And so, at this stage, he can only offer me palliative care: something to help reduce the pain and give me the energy I need to make the most of the time I have left – which he estimates to be around six months. It's May now, so that means I probably won't have to endure another Christmas. I've always hated it anyway.

Before I head back, albeit temporarily, into the land of the living, he assures me that he's done his utmost, and that in my case no decision was ever taken without his first consulting several of his esteemed colleagues; but that unfortunately there are still a few years to go before modern medicine can successfully treat every cancer.

I think that we've said everything there is to be said. Lazreg pushes his chair away from his desk and slides a lightly trembling hand through his thick grey hair. Finally, he throws his glasses down on to his notepad and stands to show me to the door.

We both pause before I leave, and he clasps my hand in his for what feels like too long. Far too long. *What does he want now?* He must have something else to tell me. I can see he's struggling to find the words. I try to pull free of his grip, but he continues to hold on.

Eventually, he spits it out. 'When it comes to palliative care . . .' he says, his voice full of empathy, yet hesitant.

'Yes?' I interrupt.

'Actually, it might just go beyond palliative. It's a new treatment. I thought I might make the trip to your house every week, so I can administer it myself.'

I have trouble hiding my surprise. This sort of undertaking must be almost unheard of.

I'm about to question his reasoning, but he anticipates me and explains, 'The drug I'm suggesting we give you hasn't yet been granted full medical approval – at least, not in Europe.'

'Oh.'

'I can get hold of it from a fellow specialist in the States, but to be quite clear, it is considered illegal.'

I detect that it's a question rather than a statement. Lazreg seems to be seeking my approval; I'm aware that bonds of mutual respect have been created between us over time, and that this is about him doing me a favour. I show him that I agree to this with a nod of the head, and ask when he's thinking of getting started.

'I'll come and see you in three days at around seven in the evening,' he replies.

At last . . . he lets go of my hand and I go home to play the waiting game.

Chapter 1

I won't be disrupting my routine in any way tonight. Some might see this as a kind of defiance: the knee-jerk reaction of a man who, knowing he is doomed, faces reality with a courage born of despair; confronts Death's imminent arrival head-on, refusing him the satisfaction of seeing him crumble . . . but that's not my style. Actually, my behaviour is down to sheer laziness.

Every night for years now I've slumped on to my sofa, beer in one hand and packet of crisps in the other, at exactly 6.50 p.m., to get my fix of my game show. I love it. For starters, it gives me a chance to take the mickey out of those morons who have the gall to show up to a TV studio with a knowledge of culture that, at best, comes from flipping through *Reader's Digest*. Plus, this is the programme where there's the most money to be won, and to be honest I find 'winning' between €100,000 and €1 million every night rather entertaining.

It's a piece of cake for me. With an IQ of 162, on top of a visual memory that astounded the droves of paediatric psychologists who examined me as a child, I am unbeatable on practically every subject you could mention. At the age of seven, for example, I'd memorised the list of prime numbers up to 100; by eleven, I knew them all the way to 1,000. I gave up when I got to 10,000 at around fourteen, as I was starting to get bored with it. Incidentally, I then went on to the Lychrel numbers, starting with the smallest candidate – 196. After 2,415,836 iterations, I'd reached a million digits without obtaining a palindrome. If I had, I think you'd have heard about it. I also learned Latin in just a few months, but that was more for fun. Contrary to what a lot of people believe, I'm not autistic and I've never been diagnosed as such; I'm simply able to answer 95 per cent of the presenters' questions correctly.

The missing 5 per cent is because I'm totally incapable of recognising a tune. If asked, I'd more than likely get the Beatles mixed up with the Rolling Stones or Bowie confused with Bob Dylan. But I'm quite confident that when it comes to literature, science or history, there's no tripping me up.

So why is it that I'm fine with sprawling out on my sofa and answering questions rather than going for some easy cash and actually taking part in one of these programmes? There are two reasons for this.

The first is that, from a very young age, this exceptionally high IQ of mine has somewhat negatively affected my social life, and the awkward gaffes I tend to make when conversing with my peers end up making me look, at best, cripplingly shy and, at worst, the village idiot – which is incredible, really, for someone with my brains. To make matters worse, and even though I've tried for many years to do something about it, I often speak using outmoded language, including expressions that have long since seen their day. Actually, I don't think I've ever sworn properly . . . not even when I'm behind the wheel. All this leads me to keep any relationships with fellow members of the human race to an absolute minimum, with only very rare exceptions, which I invariably tend to loathe.

The second reason is a lot more mundane. I no longer have any need for money. I received my BSc at fourteen and went on to obtain an MSc in applied geophysics at nineteen, before finishing up my doctoral thesis and joining the National Scientific Research Centre three years later. My salary as a researcher – alongside the courses I teach at the Institute of Astrophysics in Paris, further supplemented by my various missions at CERN in Geneva – has given me a very comfortable standard of living, and has even led to my developing some additional whims that I didn't have before.

I live at a very 'desirable' address, to quote the estate agent I dealt with at the time: thirty-three square metres in Paris's sixth arrondissement, with views overlooking the Jardin du Luxembourg. On the floor below me, there's a couple, one of whom is a TV presenter who's been on air since the invention of colour, and the other a former health minister. Upstairs there's a singer, who by all accounts is pretty famous too, but I've never heard of him. In the flat opposite, the guy's an author. Actually, he's all right – at least as all right as someone can be to my mind. There was this one time when we had what might have passed for a conversation in the entrance hall.

I felt obliged to let him know that I'd never once read one of his novels. He told me to consider myself lucky, but then gave me a copy of his bestseller. It had won some sort of prize voted for by high school students – the Goncourt, I think. He assured me that he wouldn't blame me in the least if I happened to misplace it. I did start it, though, and I even went online to read what the critics were saying so I could get a better idea as to why people liked it so much. I never dared speak to him of it again. He became a little less friendly after that episode.

I'm well aware that this neighbourhood isn't for me. Those who live here like to go out a lot – to the theatre, to official opening nights at art galleries or to film premieres. Not me. I tuck myself away in my living room, convinced of the mediocrity of the world that surrounds me and to which I believe I perhaps should never have belonged. There you have it.

Who would have thought there'd be a genius in my family? I am Régis Gaudin – the only child of Lucien Gaudin and Marie Gaudin, née Payot, who died within six months of each other fifteen years ago; Régis Gaudin, who married Corinne Lafarge just after his parents' deaths (12 June 2003, to be precise), and divorced her less than three years later without ever seeing the point in procreating, and who now lives alone and indifferent in a stunning apartment in the sixth arrondissement with his sole entertainment being to watch televised game shows. Add to this a so-so physique, softened by both a lack of exercise and deplorable eating habits – including a massive intake of crisps, beer, frozen pizzas and other junk food – plus underwhelming eyes, the charisma of a photo-booth curtain and a tendency to stammer when under emotional stress . . . and there you have the archetypal anti-hero. An anti-hero with six months of his wishy-washy life left to live.

Today's contestant is a scarily skinny sociology student. He's just gone home with €1,500 after getting stuck on a worryingly easy question: list these four Napoleonic battles in chronological order – Friedland, Trafalgar, Wagram, Marengo. It's just appalling. Surely everyone in the country knows the answer! Really, really appalling. Up next is a woman, a retired postal worker from Villeneuve-sur-Lot who tells everyone that when she plays at home in front of her TV she never gets less than €48,000. Talk about tempting fate. But before we witness her public televisual humiliation, it's the ad break. I take this opportunity to grab my tablet, which is never far from my sofa, so I can read my emails. I consider this a chore and have to force myself to do it once a day.

There's nothing exciting. A few messages from students waiting to hear what I have to say about their theses, a German colleague inviting me to the umpteenth conference on the adherence properties of gecko setæ, plus the inevitable phishing scams from a range of commercial enterprises, including a well-known insurance company offering me some sort of amazing pension scheme. Clearly, their files aren't up to date.

I postpone replying to them and turn my focus back to the programme, which is about to resume. I'm not mistaken about the fate awaiting our retired postal worker. She gets through the first two questions, which are designed solely to entertain the masses, and then starts getting the cold sweats.

'How many countries make up Great Britain?'

I just know she'll include Ireland and answer four. She starts using her fingers, a habit no doubt left over from her years counting and adding up behind her little window.

'England, Wales and Scotland and Ireland . . . four!'

What did I tell you? Back to Villeneuve-sur-Lot with you, Madame Post-Office-Woman.

One last fastest-fingers-first round – but not before an advert telling us all about the virtues of a new building material – and the programme draws to an end with the deadpan smile of the presenter.

It's the news now, so I head to the kitchen to stick a frozen lasagne in the microwave. As I watch what from a distance might just pass as real Parmesan bubble and melt, I'm surprised to find myself thinking about cremation. I will ask to be burned – of that I'm sure. There's no way I want to needlessly take up room under the earth. Then again, who would have the foolish notion to collect my ashes? What would be the point? And who should I leave these instructions with? Should I contact an undertaker now? If in doubt, do it. It's for the best. It must be part of that process traditionally referred to as 'putting your affairs in order'. I'll make sure I deal with it this week. One less thing and all that.

I stand at the edge of the work surface and shovel the lasagne into my mouth. Then I return to the sofa. There's a film on next. I try my hardest to engage with it, but it's difficult. It's about this billionaire quadriplegic who hires a black lad from the suburbs of Paris to be a home help. You couldn't get more improbable and it's deadly dull to boot. I give up, asking myself how so much money can be spent filming such rubbish.

When I switch off the TV, my living room is plunged into darkness, yet I don't feel the need to turn the set back on. I sit there feeling confused. Have I actually taken in the consequences of what I've learned today? I think so. And yet it seems impossible to me that everything can come to an end so quickly. It's too soon. There's a sense of unfinished business, although I've never really sought to accomplish anything, or if

I have it's been bits of research – work of little interest to anyone apart from a couple of fossilised scientists and other lab rats like me. It's all a bit futile, really.

I resign myself to mooching towards the room I use as my office, to see where I'm at with some of the online chess games I play with people across the globe. I only have eleven of them on the go at the moment, including one against a particularly brilliant young man called Letton, the junior world vice-champion. I think it'll end up in a draw, which is a pity. I shut down my computer just after midnight. This is when I take the sleeping pill prescribed by Professor Lazreg. For the last few weeks it's been impossible to sleep without it. There's only one tablet left in the packet. I mustn't forget to go to the chemist's tomorrow.

Chapter 2

Upon waking, I have a little difficulty getting my thoughts together. Yes, of course: the first thing to cross my mind is my imminent demise. For several days, perhaps even several weeks, I've been under no illusion. I know I'm doomed, but I did think that getting the confirmation from my doctor would provoke a greater fear – a violent reaction, or a panic attack at the very least. There's nothing of the sort. I obey the autopilot that forces me to get out of bed, take a shower and eat two croissants out of the packet, dipping them into a mug of instant coffee while watching a rolling news channel.

The weatherman announces that it's the first real day of spring. Today is 24 May, so it's about time. As I spend hours and hours in front of a screen – whether my television or my computer – I have no real reason to rejoice in this information, but it does all feel slightly different this morning. If nothing had changed, I'd be hunched over one of the awaiting theses on my desk or immersed in the latest recorded data from the accelerator at Stanford. But not today. In a break from all usual patterns, I grab a jacket from my wardrobe, something lighter than I'd normally wear, and head outside. As soon as I step out on to the pavement, however, I perform an about-turn and run back upstairs to change my slippers for a pair of moccasins.

I walk the length of the pavement outside the Jardin du Luxembourg, but I'm hesitant to enter. I've been living with this park beneath my windows for twelve years and I haven't yet set foot in it, not even when it would make sense to walk through it as a shortcut. I observe it from my flat sometimes. The trees let me in on what season it is, but that's about it. The thought occurs to me that it might not be that unpleasant to amble along its pathways before they're invaded by screaming kids.

Through the wrought-iron fencing I see a young woman on her morning jog. She's approaching me. Her tread is light and graceful. Unlike most of the health-and-fitness types who partake in this sport, she actually looks to be enjoying herself; she's smiling under her baseball cap. As she passes, she gives me a little wave. By the time I realise what has just happened and turn to see who she might have been greeting, she has disappeared behind a bush. I don't need to look in a mirror to know that there must have been some sort of misunderstanding. I'm not the kind of person people wave at unless they're obliged to. Could she be one of my students? Given how many of them there are, I can't commit all their faces to memory, and anyway, it's been some time since I was last in an auditorium. On reflection, it's not possible. She was young – a lot younger than me – but not quite young enough to still be attending lectures at the Institute of Astrophysics. There must be some rational explanation. Of course! She confused me for an acquaintance. That must have been it.

As I convince myself of this, I arrive at the bottom of Rue de Fleurus. I ready myself for the adventure that is making my way across the Jardin du Luxembourg – no easy task for me – but end up changing my mind. This is nothing to do with anxiety, but because I have another idea. I want to take a stroll alongside the cemetery at Montparnasse, where there are a number of undertakers. Is that a weird idea? Morbid? Not really. I may as well get all this boring business out of the way before my physical condition goes ahead and deteriorates. At least this way, I'll avoid any poorly acted compassion from the undertaker's staff. And it might just be that preparing the funeral service will help me come to terms with the reality of my expiry date. Who knows?

It takes me less than twenty minutes to find what I'm looking for. I spot two shopfronts and choose the smaller of them. The larger place is much more eye-catching and gives the impression of being much more luxurious, but it's far too over-the-top for me. And more than anything else, I can see who would be dealing with me – a young man, very tall, very sure of himself, who would, I'm absolutely sure of it, have me agreeing to his every suggestion. I know how I am when I come across people like this: I'm totally incapable of refusing anything they attempt to sell me. That's exactly how I found myself suddenly the owner of a brand-new six-cylinder Audi estate when I'd gone out to buy a Polo. So, no, not him. However, I've already walked past the other shop three times and haven't yet seen anyone inside. Who am I going to be faced with? Never mind. I'm going to go for it.

A woman welcomes me. Bad news. My dealings with male acquaintances are already complicated enough and, of course, it's a whole lot worse with the opposite sex. But she's well over fifty and I don't find her particularly attractive in her grey woollen dress and black fitted jacket. I should be able to keep my wits about me. However, she's already seated behind her desk, which I hadn't noticed from outside, so she must have seen me walking back and forth in front of the window and taken me for a nutcase. Well, I'll soon find out.

'Sir? Can I help you at all?'

Her voice is warm and full of empathy. She must have learned how to do that at funeral school.

'Perhaps. Actually, I'd like some information in order to make some provisions for . . . an upcoming death.'

'Of course. That's what we're here for. Please take a seat.'

I sit down in the leather chair facing her desk. There are coffin catalogues arranged in front of me. That's another thing I'm going to have to decide on. Even though I want to be thrown into the fire as soon as they put me in it, I bet it's mandatory to have one.

'So . . . I imagine this is for someone close to you?'

'Erm, yes . . . I don't think we could be any closer.'

What has got into me, to say such a thing? As if it all isn't complicated enough, I'm now putting myself in an even more embarrassing situation.

'A parent?' she asks.

'Uh . . . no. In fact . . . it's for me.'

'Oh . . . well, that's quite a different matter, then.'

'Why? Is it not the done thing?'

'No! It's not that. Actually, it makes sense. The loss of a loved one is already painful enough for a family. If we can help them with the management of certain obligations ahead of time, we're doing them a huge favour. Now then . . .'

'Yes?'

There is a hint of awkwardness behind her reassuring speech. It takes her a few seconds to find the words to continue.

'It's more often than not elderly clients who take these steps, but if you're here today, it's possibly because you're afraid . . .'

'Quite right. I've got six months. At best. At least, that's what my doctor told me yesterday,' I say with a nervous laugh.

Yet another example of my inability to communicate normally with my fellow man (or woman, for that matter). I hope she doesn't think I'm having her on.

'I'm so sorry to hear that,' she nevertheless assures me.

She must be putting my awkwardness down to emotional shock following my very recent bad news.

At this point, I may as well get to the bottom line. 'The bottom line' is the exact term I use to talk about cremation with her. She continues as if this is all quite standard practice, and busies herself with questions as to whether I've consulted my family, as apparently some people still have problems accepting cremation as a final choice. When I explain to her that I have no close relatives with whom I can share this decision, that presumably I'll have to inform the hospital staff and that they'll be in touch when the time comes, her compassion strikes me as being sincere. As for the ashes, it's she who suggests having them placed in the cemetery where my parents are buried. It's in Charentes, the same village where they bought a little house for their retirement. But neither of them made it as far as retiring. Maybe it's some sort of family tradition.

Following a few more fairly innocent-sounding questions whose sole purpose is to uncover my budget, she promises to send me an estimate within the week. I should be able to last that long.

I feel relieved as soon as I leave the place. It was something that I had to get out of the way, and now it's done. There is no big wave of emotion, despite having discussed exactly what would become of me after my departure. I haven't really grasped my situation any better, but I believe I dealt with all that very well. This is quite rare for me.

I feel not only a sense of relief – I also feel quite well. Two months ago, I was put through some pretty heavy radiotherapy and it left me in a sorry state indeed. It would have been unthinkable back then for me to have walked as far as I have today; I could only just about manage to take the lift down to the ground floor and climb into the taxi that took me to hospital. Little by little, I started to feel better, and today I'm more than capable of making my way home on foot. I even decide that I can complete this morning's mission: a walk in the Jardin du Luxembourg.

I stroll down the main pathway in the direction of the Sénat. It's a beautiful sight. It really is. A few random memories drift back to me. A school trip in particular. My so-called 'chums' – as we referred to each other back then – pushed me into the park lake. It came as no surprise to our teacher, as he was so used to me being bullied. I was the official class whipping-boy. I had to go home, soaked to the bone, to be welcomed by a pitying yet resigned look from my mother.

You can still hire miniature boats here: colourful old sailboats that children can push around the edge of the lake with sticks. It's surprising that they should still want to do this in the age of virtual-reality helmets connected to smartphones.

I walk around the lake, then along, parallel to Boulevard Saint-Michel, as far as the Medici Fountain. I think about my neighbour's novel again. I can't remember the title and didn't even get through a third of it, but I seem to remember this fountain playing an important role in the storyline. The main character used to sit here and read with his girlfriend. Or something like that.

Polyphemus surprising Acis and Galatea

I perhaps didn't understand a word of that novel, but I have a perfect memory when it comes to the story behind this fountain. As was systematic with me as a child, on that very first school trip to the park, I learned what was written on the plaque in front of the monument by heart. We must have taken the tour in the opposite direction, because it was before I ended up in the lake.

I'm just checking that my memory is still up to scratch by rereading the plaque when she suddenly comes up behind me.

'Hello.'

As I turn, I recognise the baseball cap with its wide visor and, underneath it, the young woman who waved at me earlier this morning. She's thirty – maybe thirty-five – with sparkling blue eyes and a few strands of black hair falling over her face. She must have stopped running a while ago because she's not the slightest bit out of breath.

'Erm, yes . . . Hello.'

'I'm sorry about this morning. I could tell straight away that you didn't recognise me. Especially dressed like this . . .'

She stretches out her leg, points to her tracksuit bottoms and pulls at her T-shirt with her other hand, accentuating the baggy effect. It looks to me like she's someone who doesn't take herself too seriously. I get the feeling that I might even think she's quite nice. But who is she?

'I don't want you to take this the wrong way,' I venture timidly, 'but I don't think we've ever met. Are you a student of mine?'

'I wish!' She laughs. 'It'd make me a good few years younger than I am, but no.' Her face takes on a more serious expression as she adds, 'We bumped into one another at the hospital. Several times, in fact. Sorry, I thought you . . . Well, excuse me, then . . . I just . . .'

'No, it is me,' I interrupt eagerly. 'I just don't recall faces well.'

It's no good trying to pretend I recognise her now. I won't come across as very credible. And I can't just walk off either, without at least showing a minimum of interest.

'So have you been ill, then?'

'No, I was visiting someone.' She seems hesitant. This is always such a delicate subject. 'You look a lot better than when I last saw you there. Are you . . . on the right track?'

I already find it difficult to talk about with the few people I know properly, so I'm not about to start spouting off to a near-stranger. 'It's too soon. We don't really know.'

'Ah . . .'

This is verging on uncomfortable now, and I've had more than enough emotion for one morning. 'It's . . . it's been a pleasure. Goodbye now.'

I make a swift getaway without daring to turn back. I'd rather not imagine what she might think of me.

CHAPTER 3

The rest of the day plays out in a way that conforms a lot more closely to my usual habits. After another warmed-up frozen meal eaten straight out of the packet and a short nap, I spend three hours straight on a thesis with so much wrong with it that I start to fear my own scientific and pedagogical abilities, followed by a couple of games of chess and a trip to the kitchen to fish around in the beer drawer in the fridge. When I throw myself down on to my sofa, it is with an almost child-like feeling of having spent the first day of the rest of my life achieving something useful.

I'm impatiently watching the titles roll to *Who Wants to Be a Millionaire?* when there's an event that hasn't occurred since the bin men came around selling their Christmas calendars last November. Someone knocks at my door.

It's her again. She's changed her clothes and instead of sportswear she's now wearing turned-up jeans, shabby trainers and a scuffed leather jacket. She's not exactly the epitome of elegance. She remains quite pretty, however, and even dressed as she is, she doesn't lack for charm.

As she stands there in the hallway, it suddenly dawns on me. She's going to ask me if I read the Bible. That must be it. My first reflex tells me to shut the door in her face, but I think better of it pretty quickly because, no . . . she's not dressed like a Jehovah's Witness or any of those other evangelical Bible-bashers.

As I dither, she grabs her chance and confidently thrusts out her hand to me. 'I didn't introduce myself earlier. Chloé Schneider. Schneider like the actress. Romy? You know? Delighted to see you again.'

I reply instinctively, and before I'm able to ask to what I owe the honour, she takes the initiative and starts a conversation.

'Monsieur Gaudin, I'm afraid I lied to you a bit this morning. I'm fully aware of the dreadful news you've just been given, and I'd like to talk to you.'

This can't be right. What does this woman want with me? Unless . . . I've heard that some of those cancer charities are very quick off the mark when it comes to making the most of loved ones' generosity when people die, and that family members are particularly receptive just after they lose someone; but to think they get right down to work before someone's even dead, and go after the dying people themselves . . . Well, it's something I'd never have the courage to do. But she doesn't allow me the time to express my feelings on the matter because she just keeps talking.

'I know that you only have six months left to live, and I'm here to give you the last adventure this life has to offer . . . or, dare I say, the only adventure your life has ever offered?'

'Is that right? And what is this offer of yours? Should I sail around the world? Take a trip to the moon? It's my pleasure to inform you that I'm not into that kind of business!' I try my hardest to adopt a sarcastic tone, but it doesn't sound at all right coming from me.

My visitor's smile expands. 'Don't worry! I understand that you're more the stay-at-home type. The actual reason I'm here is to ask for your assistance in killing a couple of people. Can I come in?'

She explains this in such a way that, even without her charming smile, I think I'd let her invade my space. I move to one side and usher her in.

She takes a seat on the sofa. I drag my large wing chair over to the coffee table so I can sit facing her. She seems to be expecting something from me and, for once, I respond fairly rapidly. I start by turning off the television and then, in accordance with the social niceties to which I am so ill accustomed, I offer her something to drink. In this case, it's beer, coffee . . . or nothing. A quick trip to the kitchen produces a bottle of 1664, which I place down on the table next to my own, along with a glass, which she pushes to one side. She lifts the bottle towards me as if to make a toast before taking a first gulp. I imitate her gesture and do my best to put on a cheerful air, like a man who's at ease no matter what the circumstances, the sort who has a witty response to any given situation.

'So perhaps you'd like to start by telling me who it is you'd like me to do away with?'

My inept sense of humour is really something. Her face remains closed, but her eyes scrutinise me. She must be wondering whether or not she knocked on the right door.

I'm obliged to apologise for my tone. I ask her again, more seriously this time, if she can explain why she's come to see me.

Her mocking smile returns, and tiny wrinkles appear around her eyes. Ridiculous though it seems, I do find her very attractive. I try to force the thought from my mind.

'Régis . . . Can I call you Régis?' she asks without waiting for a response. 'Please understand that the offer I'm putting on the table tonight is as serious as they come. Obviously, it isn't exactly what you'd call conventional and perhaps it doesn't conform to everyone's idea of morality, but it is nonetheless very serious.'

I nod to show I've got the message loud and clear and that I won't attempt any further irony.

She continues. 'Let me put this simply. I'm an agent working with a small group of people who got together quite unintentionally following what we might refer to as "tragic accidents". Now . . . I'm not going to go into all the details with you, but let's just say that each of the members of our "association", which of course doesn't have any kind of official status, has lived through one or more painful events that have led them to view life quite differently from others, and to consider some people's continued existence to be perhaps not what we'd call "fair".'

She pauses to make sure I've fully grasped the no-nonsense nature of the subject, and then resumes her speech. 'I want to get a possible misunderstanding out of the way from the outset. We're not simply looking for a hitman to settle a couple of scores.'

'Well, that's the impression you're giving, from what you've said so far,' I say before I can stop myself.

'I get that. But that's just it. I don't think I've explained myself properly. What I mean is the people I'll suggest you help me eliminate pose a threat to society as a whole. Once we get to work, you'll see that these are people nobody will miss. Their disappearance will bring about either total indifference or even a sigh of relief from the vast majority of the population. Are you getting this now? It's important that you do before I let you in on the rest of our project.'

Our project . . . I note that I'm actually in the middle of having a fairly pleasant discussion about my future as a murderer, as if it's something I've done all my life, and as if this is nothing more than a new contract in which we'll be adding a few names to my already long list of victims. I pull myself together and try to look pensive.

'Do you have any idea what you're talking about? You've said it's a noble cause and that these assassinations can be justified . . . but do you actually believe I'm the right man for the job? If so, it's quite evident you don't know me at all.'

'But I do!' she retorts with a fit of laughter. 'And better than you might think!'

'Is that so? Then you'll know I'm a researcher. A scientist who lives as a recluse in his flat, someone who's more or less totally disconnected from society . . . someone who's been described as asocial and who has only half a year to live.'

'I know all that. And a lot more.'

'Not to mention the fact that, despite the aversion I have to a great many aspects of our society, I've never really veered off what you'd call the straight and narrow. I've never broken the law. Nor my own moral code, for that matter.'

'I know that about you, too.'

'So you're mad, then!'

'Not at all. You must follow my logic. Only someone in your position would consider accepting this offer. Firstly, if I'm to avoid police suspicion of any kind, I need someone who hasn't got so much as a speeding ticket. That's you. Secondly, the fewer familial or romantic attachments the person has, the freer they'll be to get the job done. And, if I'm not mistaken, you also fit the bill perfectly there . . . Finally, I need someone who has nothing to lose. And, as it happens . . .'

She has trouble finishing her sentence. She grabs her beer, but it doesn't go anywhere near her mouth. She's holding it for confidence.

'I don't believe for a second it would happen,' she continues, 'but if you end up getting arrested, not only would you not have to deal with being banged up for years, but because of the state of your health you'd be given more flexible living conditions inside. I'm not even convinced you'd be detained while it went to trial and regrettably, if you'll excuse me, you wouldn't live long enough to see a courtroom.'

'Honestly! Single men unknown to the police and with death sentences hanging over them can't be all that hard to come by. And some of them must be more suited to this kind of work.'

'Don't be so modest,' she replies. It's now clear she's taking great pleasure in our discussion. 'I understand you a lot better than you'd believe, and I know you possess quite a few qualities that are indispensable to our project.'

'Really? Can you name them?'

'Well, I know that you've been working with psychiatrists on how to control your feelings since you were very young. You've learned to master your emotions like no one else.'

She's right about that. I am hyperactive, hypersensitive, hyper-emotional – and I now know how to extract myself mentally from what I deem to be an unstable situation in order to protect my psyche. But how does she know that? It's a mystery.

'So what?' I come back with. 'Do you think the whole aim was to make me fit for killing people?'

'Of course not! On the other hand, you can't really deny that it has helped you put up a front under stress.'

She's forging ahead here – perhaps a step too far – because right now I'm about to lose it and show her the door, as my intuition told me to do from the outset. What holds me back is the desire to ask her how she found all this out about me.

But she won't be interrupted. 'And then there's your unbelievable IQ. I must make you aware that the missions we have to accomplish are beyond the reach of most. We need people who can stay sharp and on their guard. If these "assassinations", and that is the right word, are to be correctly conducted, we're going to have to come up with a real strategy, act with complete discretion and overcome all obstacles in our path. This is an amazing challenge I'm throwing your way, which is why I referred to it as the adventure of a lifetime.'

The adventure of a lifetime . . . What is this? If she really has delved into who I am, she should know that I like nothing better than shutting myself away in my flat and keeping my relationships with others to the bare minimum; also, that I see any trips or experiences that force me out of my daily routine as challenges that are becoming increasingly difficult to overcome.

'Before we go any further, where did you get all this information about me?'

'I know you must be surprised, even worried,' she replies. 'But please don't view this as some sort of intrusion into your private life. These are details that certain . . . let's say . . . "departments" keep on all our citizens. I won't be telling you any more about the structure of our organisation. All you need to know is that we boast colossal financial means, an excellent network, and that several of our members occupy extraordinarily high governmental positions.'

Is she trying to impress me? If so, she's failed. I'm more than aware that the work I do can have massive repercussions on the powers that be. They didn't give me free rein over what happens at CERN without first assuring themselves of my trustworthiness and, of course, I had to supply them with a great deal of personal information before being given access to both national and international works-in-progress. But none of that matters anyway. It's about time I let her know she's way off track with me. She needs to leave me in peace to watch the end of *Who Wants to Be a Millionaire?* As if reading my thoughts, she starts coming up with responses to things I haven't even said out loud.

'I know that the word "adventure" in the strict sense isn't exactly your cup of tea. But back when you were completing your studies, and even throughout your career, you've always enjoyed a challenge or finding solutions to problems that were beyond the understanding of your colleagues. So just think about my proposition from that angle. It's an enigma that needs to be solved. It's just that you can't get caught solving it. Please believe me when I tell you that you're going to love it.'

I'm about to get up, draw this discussion to its conclusion and show her the way out when one of the points she's raised pops back into my head.

'You said something about having a lot of "means". Perhaps I should ask how much I could expect to earn from this offer of yours?'

The young woman smiles at me with the compassion that befits the situation. 'Régis, you can't hide the fact . . . and I know perfectly well anyway . . . that there's nobody you need to look after . . . plus you have all the money you need to live very comfortably for what time you have left. No, I have nothing to offer you but an intense emotional ride and the feeling of having accomplished something great before taking leave of this world. You can trust me. Accept my offer. You won't regret it.'

I'm wondering whether this is a wind-up of some kind – a stitch-up. But who would do that? Who out of the few acquaintances I have would embark on a hoax like this? I don't believe it. It's out of the question. It is, however, highly likely that I'm in the presence of a lunatic. Which is a pity. Because I thought she was rather nice . . . Funny, even. Not to mention pleasing to the eye. Maybe, under a different set of circumstances, I could have made an effort to be sociable, or even had a go at the risky business of chatting her up.

But reason prevails, and I stand up for good this time, inviting her to do the same. She gets to her feet with visible regret. Once standing, she pulls out a brown envelope from inside her jacket and places it down on the coffee table.

'I'll be off, Régis. But I'm going to leave this file with you. It concerns the first person we have to kill. Read it. Perhaps it'll help change your mind. There's also my telephone number in there. You can get hold of me any time, day or night.'

She finally moves in the direction of the front door, but turns back to face me. 'At least admit that you have trouble finding any kind of affinity with people, and that if the worst should happen to some of them you'd be more likely to rejoice than anything else.'

I quicken my step, overtake her and stand by the door. Before I can open it, Chloé Schneider smirks at me again and I detect a touch of self-importance.

'Obviously, if you're thinking of calling the police, I didn't give you my real name and the phone number in the file is for a prepaid mobile. If you try to describe me, rest assured you'll get nowhere on that front either.' She pauses – perhaps for the drama of it – before giving me one last smile. 'And even if you did contact them, they'd have to take you seriously and to be quite honest . . .'

I try to remain courteous as I place my hand lightly on her back and nudge her into the corridor outside, but she still has the gall to add a gentle threat.

'Don't waste time thinking about this. I have to act now, and if you continue to refuse to work with us, I'll have to get down to finding someone more . . . cooperative.'

I don't hang around to watch her leave, but as she steps into the lift I swear I see her giving herself the thumbs-up in the interior mirror. As if she thinks she has this one in the bag . . .

Chapter 4

The next few days pass very quickly. Just as I did on that first night following the news of my sentence, I try to stick to my routine. I watch a lot of television and I spend hours on the web looking up the latest goings-on in the scientific world. The Large Hadron Collider in Geneva has just been put back into service after a long period of scheduled maintenance and I'm waiting with bated breath to see what data it comes up with next. Every time a new collision takes place, I stay up late into the night working on a new flood of calculations. I follow this same itinerary all week – except on Tuesday.

I have to switch the computer off earlier than usual that day, because that's when Professor Lazreg comes.

He arrives at around 7 p.m., as arranged, and is very considerate towards me. He asks how I'm feeling, and I explain that, apart from a few episodes where I've felt very tired, things have been going rather well. He examines me briefly before going ahead with the injection. As he presses the plunger on the syringe, he warns me that the next twelve hours may prove to be a little taxing; he recommends, even though he doesn't wish to deprive me of the slightest thing at the moment, that I avoid too much alcohol during this time.

I get the strange feeling that Professor Lazreg is in no hurry to leave. I even imagine that, should I dare ask, he would be happy to sit down and have a beer with me. But he doesn't have the nerve to start up a conversation either, even though I sense that he would like to question me more about my day-to-day life and how I'm learning to live with the news he gave me last week.

One morning, I find myself paused with my spoon hovering above my coffee cup, wondering what I could feasibly change about my mundane existence for the six months I have left. Nothing comes to me. Not even a hint of an idea. And so I remain either curled up in bed, or collapsed on my sofa, or hunched over my desk in my office having found the answer to yet another polytropic process equation.

I am deep in thought when, driven by I know not what (probably scientific curiosity), I pick up the brown envelope left for me by the somewhat puzzling Chloé Schneider. I see a name: Grégoire Thule. This man is known to have murdered a little girl, Lilian . . . but is also presumed to have committed several rapes and to be responsible for a number of unexplained disappearances. A copy of his ID sits alongside a very full file, in which I read that he is going to be leaving the high-security prison in Aiton down in Savoie and be hospitalised in Lyon for bone marrow treatment, which it is hoped will save him from the leukaemia ravaging his body. I also find a plan of the hospital and directions to the intensive care room he is expected to occupy for three weeks following his surgery. The operation is due to take place within a fortnight, after an extensive battery of medical tests that are set to start on Tuesday, the day after his transfer from prison in an armoured police vehicle.

I don't have the foggiest clue as to whether this information is reliable. I return the papers to the envelope and throw it back down on to the table. Nor do I check to see if the promised phone number is contained within the file.

Seven days following my first injection, Professor Lazreg is back at my place. He starts off by asking me how the first few hours went after his last visit. I confirm that I felt enormously tired that evening – until the next morning, in fact – but that the rest of the week has gone by without a hitch.

Again, he gives me a quick examination. And again, I feel like he'd rather stay than go home. So I take the bull by the horns and ask if he'd like a drink. He accepts with eagerness but refuses a beer, saying that he never drinks alcohol. He seems happy enough with a glass of water. I am, however, a little taken aback when, once seated, he says, 'I'm absolutely delighted to be able to sit down and talk properly.'

'Is there a problem that falls outside the scope of our normal consultations that you wish to discuss?' I ask, encouraging him with a smile.

'I wouldn't use the word *problem*. It's just that . . .'

I'm really not expecting this attitude from my doctor. He is usually so sure of himself but appears awkward now, at a loss for words or at least loath to speak them.

In the end, I have to almost give him permission to get it off his chest. 'Go ahead, Professor. I don't know what you could possibly tell me that is any worse than what we already know.'

This must be the right way to go about it, because he starts now with more self-assurance. 'Well, obviously, this still concerns the state of your health. Unfortunately, you're not the first person to whom I've had to give such a diagnosis, and nor will you be the last. But what usually happens is that my colleagues and I refer our patients to a psychiatrist almost immediately. And they help them with their preparations. This allows us to concentrate on other patients . . . with whom we hope to be more effective.'

I appreciate his frankness. I didn't get the impression that this was what he was doing when he suggested I go and 'see someone' at the hospital, but upon reflection that's what it boiled down to. 'I've done what I can,' he'd said. 'It hasn't worked, and I'm sorry. Please go and see Dr So-and-So, who will help you get through this.'

Tough luck for him and his conscience, though, because I'd refused to go and see Dr So-and-So. I had no desire whatsoever to lie down on a chaise-longue and tell someone my life story. Or my death story.

'And is it because I neglected to go that you felt the need to come up with the idea of these injections? Are you checking on the state of my morale?'

I don't speak with any aggression, but he must think I'm angry because as he replies he has something of a confused smile on his lips.

'Something like that, I must admit. But let's also say that yours is a special case.'

'Why's that?'

'It's as I said. I'm regularly confronted with this, but not all my patients react in the same way. Some become very quickly resigned to their fate, whereas others feel outrage at the injustice of it all. I even have certain patients who seem very much at peace with it. But with you . . . it's unfathomable. I'm totally incapable of interpreting how you've taken the news. You don't let your feelings show at all. And that's why I'm so worried about you and may come across as so heavy-handed when I ask how things are.'

I pick up my 1664 and clink it against his glass of water. What I want to do with this gesture is to thank him for his concern, but I can't verbalise it. I take a sip. He follows suit and the pair of us try to regain some composure.

It doesn't work, and I gingerly start to speak. 'I don't think I could even begin to tell you where I'm at with all this.'

'Please try.'

'Erm . . . Well, I know I'm going to die in the not-so-distant future. It's what I keep telling myself, anyway. But I suppose I don't feel all that bothered about it. It's just a simple fact.'

'And are you sure you've taken on board what that actually means?'

'I think so, yes.'

'And you say it's something you repeatedly tell yourself? Is that maybe because you need to convince yourself of it? Do you think that might be so?'

To humour him, I take some time to think about his question. But it all seems very clear from my standpoint. Yes, in six months' time, I'll be dead. I'll have left a world I never asked to be part of. And this world isn't exactly a bundle of laughs, is it? Whatever happens, the particle accelerator will continue to turn at 0.999999991 times the speed of light, game show contestants will still make fools of themselves in front of the nation, and as for me, my ashes will turn into fertiliser for plants as a small link in the great food chain. My journey on this earth will have come to an end, and if we work on the basis of the average lifespan of a man of my generation, my time here will have been cut short by 36.7 years. Big deal.

But I know that Professor Lazreg wouldn't believe any of this if I said it out loud. It wouldn't add up. It's another example of my non-standard behaviour – something I've been told about regularly over the last forty years. For now, he stares at me with a look of great empathy.

'A few years ago,' he says gently, 'I had a patient who didn't react at all when I announced that the treatment had failed. She just carried on with life as if there was nothing wrong, and told everyone around her to stop worrying. She didn't make a single change. She went on working as long as she was able and when her time came, her husband would later tell me, her final words before losing consciousness and coming to a quiet end were, "So it was true, then . . ." Can you imagine? This woman stayed in denial for every moment left to her.'

'And do you think it's the same with me?'

'I have no idea. What I do know is that I hope it's not the case. The reason behind this anecdote is that I'm convinced that, at that very last moment, this patient of mine must have regretted not doing what needed to be done before her end.'

'Do you mean she didn't take the time to tell her children and her husband that she loved them? I thought you understood that none of that applies to me.'

He cuts me off by raising a hand. 'Yes, I know you're a single man. I don't know what this other patient might have wanted to do. Maybe it was to tell those close to her that she loved them, or it could have been any number of things. That's not the point. All I know is that she refused to accept the truth and that she went with a feeling of unfinished business. And I think that's one of the worst things that can happen to us: death coming for us, whether we're old or not so old, and we haven't accomplished what we were destined to do.'

I listen attentively, and even though I'm surprised at the way he's going about this, I'm starting to get what he's saying. After his heartfelt speech, he finishes off his glass of water, masking his flushed cheeks with his hands. I offer him another, but he politely refuses.

'I'm expected elsewhere tonight, but if you want I could rearrange my diary next week and we could continue this discussion.'

'It would be my pleasure,' I hear myself reply, a little unwillingly.

We both stand up and walk towards the door. As we step into the entrance hall, he stops to look at a photo – the only one of me in the entire flat. It was taken at the launch of the *Ariane* rocket in Kourou, Guyana. In my hands, I'm holding a medal awarded to me by the European Space Agency for my participation in the mission.

'Have you travelled a lot?' he asks me, not taking his eyes off the picture.

'Very little. That was the first time I'd ever been on a plane and I have dreadful memories of it. When I was still working for them, I had to go to Geneva regularly, but I would take the train. I always managed to find a way to refuse to go to conferences that were too far away.'

'You're afraid of flying?'

'Yes, sort of. Actually, it's not just that. Let's just say I'm not really at ease when close proximity to others is foisted upon me. And I don't really like changes in my environment either. That's all. Why do you ask?'

He turns to face me and gives a weak shrug of his shoulders. 'Because it can be that, too. Before dying, you could regret never having seen New York, the Great Pyramids or Ha Long Bay.'

I let out a laugh that sounds a little too forced. 'You're determined for me to find something I want to do before I pass on, aren't you?'

'I think it would be a good idea, yes. At least, it might be worth a moment's thought. Should we speak about it again next week?'

'I can't promise you anything, but we can still have a drink together if you want. I can get some fruit juice in or something fizzy between now and then?'

'I'm perfectly happy with water,' he says, smiling. 'Have a lovely evening.'

Once I've closed the door I just stand there for a few seconds, my arms swinging, wondering whether to return to my computer or head back to the sofa and the TV. The news is coming on shortly and for once I decide to pay it some attention; but not without first going to the fridge for another beer so I can face the litany of bad news in good company.

This is the opening headline: '*Grégoire Thule, the man infamously incarcerated following the murder of Lilian Dupres and presumed to have committed crimes against other minors, has survived an attempted assassination in his hospital room in Lyon. The shooter himself was killed by police gunfire when trying to make his escape with a female nurse he had taken hostage. His identity has not yet been made public. Nor his motivation. However, investigators suspect . . .*'

I stare at the screen without listening to what follows. I have an image in my head of the young woman who came to this very flat not ten days ago. Is this a coincidence? I mean, there must be a lot of people out there who want to see a man like him dead. Should I conclude that she was serious? That she found some other desperate man after I refused to do her bidding? This also leads me to believe that she'll be on the hunt for someone new now that the poor soul she managed to convince is no longer of use to her.

I hesitate for a few seconds, and then my blood suddenly starts pounding. Where in the heck did I put that damned envelope? I scan the coffee table, remembering I'd wanted to throw it away and then thought it wiser to burn it. But I don't remember doing that. I rush through to my office and shuffle through the ever-present pile of papers on my desk. There it is, between one of the thousand social security receipts and my latest pay slip from the Institute of Astrophysics.

I carefully remove each sheet from the envelope. It's on the last piece of paper that I find the mobile number she mentioned. I hesitate for yet another few seconds before consulting the rest of the documents. Among others, there's a plan of the hospital and a photo of this Grégoire Thule. I go and look for my phone.

Chapter 5

'Hello, Régis. I'm delighted to hear from you.'

I'd secretly hoped that she wouldn't pick up and that I could leave her a message. No such luck. Now I have to find the right formal greeting, or at least an opening topic of conversation, no matter how banal; but nothing comes to me, so I make do with a direct order.

'Explain yourself.'

At the other end of the line I hear a light laugh, which helps me to imagine her. She must be at home. I have an image of a chic interior, like something out of a homes-and-gardens magazine – the on-trend vintage look. Whatever it looks like, it'll be nothing like my flat, which I've decorated any which way without the first thought to style. She lives alone, too. But probably not for the same reasons I do.

'If you've decided to call me back,' she says in a sarcastic tone, 'then you've already understood.'

'Perhaps. But I'd like to hear your version. Just to see if it matches my own.'

'Not on the phone, though. Let's say your place in half an hour?'

With what I know, or what I think I know, I am not inclined to have her over to my flat. When all is said and done, this woman, who I first took to be so kind and bright, is now starting to seriously worry me – intimidate me, even.

'I'd rather meet elsewhere. Nine o'clock outside Saint-Sulpice church?'

'As you wish. See you later.'

When I get there, there are a couple of yuppie types making the most of the warm spring evening to go for a run. Sitting in front of the church are three homeless men drinking wine straight from the bottle, surrounded by a small pack of dogs. Chloé is standing at a short distance. She is dressed a lot more elegantly than she was when she visited my place. Her short tailored jacket gives off an air-hostess vibe. Her hair looks better styled than it did, and she's applied her make-up tastefully. She gives me a frank smile by way of greeting and assures me that she's very pleased to see me. Once the niceties are out of the way, she suggests we continue our conversation somewhere a little more discreet, and her eyes scan the edges of the square.

'Any ideas?'

'Come,' I say to her, turning and walking back towards the Jardin du Luxembourg.

There are only thirty minutes left before they close the gates for the night. I have no trouble finding a little bench set back from the main pathway, where a number of pedestrians are still making their way through the park. A wannabe poet has engraved on the wood that a certain Salomé is his muse and inspiration. I sit down to one side of this declaration and invite Chloé to take a seat beside me. She is wearing the same triumphant grin that I seem to remember noting when she left my apartment.

'Were you surprised?' she asks me playfully, as I sit there trying to find a way to break the ice.

I can't think of an answer. I don't really want her to know that yes, I was surprised – astonished, even.

I tread carefully. 'So you're saying it was you who made an attempt on that rapist's life?'

Her smile disappears, and in its place I see an affronted grimace. 'Of course it was me! Did you doubt it? You obviously didn't take me seriously, then?'

'Please understand,' I reply weakly. 'You turn up at my place to tell me that there are a number of people you want to get rid of and that you'll need my help. I don't think many people receive visitors quite like you. You must admit, I was bound to wonder if it was some kind of joke.'

'And now?'

'Now, I think I'm more inclined to believe you . . . even though there's still room for an element of doubt.'

'What more do you need?'

'If this man did what he was charged with, you could well imagine that the father of one of those poor kids decided to take things into his own hands.'

I'm not expecting her to take this well, but I get quite the opposite reaction. Her eyes start to shine again.

'Have you been told the identity of the person who committed this attempted murder?'

I stare at her for a moment before understanding where she's going with this.

'No,' I admit. 'They said on the news that his identity hasn't been confirmed.'

'I think it will remain undisclosed for a few days to come, but I can assure you that before tomorrow morning they'll announce that the man was ex-army, aged thirty-nine and originally from Poland. They might also let on that he was a drug addict suffering from AIDS. Later on, everyone will learn that he was one Tomasz Olech. Anything else?'

'Yes. Where were you when it happened?'

'I was at the wheel of an ambulance in front of the accident and emergency department at the hospital, waiting to get our man out of there after the execution.' There's the triumphant grin again.

I make it disappear as quickly as it arrived by reminding her of the terrible outcome. 'Hmm . . . A hostage got taken, your man was shot dead and your target is still alive, so I'd hardly call the operation a success.'

'I wasn't expecting a miracle either,' she says in a defensive tone. 'I was under a lot of pressure from my . . . well . . . from the people in the group when I was choosing the guy. He reckoned he was some kind of elite soldier but honestly, I never really thought he'd be up to scratch. Big head, small brain. That's all he was.'

A park-keeper makes his way towards us. We lapse into silence as he approaches. When he reaches our bench, he reminds us that the gardens will close very shortly, and I reassure him that we're just about to leave.

Chloé waits until he's moved on before adding in a whisper, 'That's why I need you! If I have to deal with his kind again, not only will I not achieve anything but there's a chance I'll get arrested into the bargain.'

She pauses before offering me a self-mocking but humorous look. 'And that would be a shame, don't you think?'

A whistle sounds, signalling that it's time to leave. She ignores it and continues pleading with me as we walk. 'Now you know exactly what went down. What would you have done?'

Rather than telling her clearly where to go, which as a more or less balanced human being I should do, I start considering her question. Without having taken a close look at the plan of the hospital, I try to imagine the site. A sterile room isolated from the other wards, with extremely controlled access and, in the case of this particular man, police presence.

'I don't think I would have tried my luck in his room, you know. Maybe I'd have had a go while he was being transferred, or done it in the room they put people in immediately after surgery. And I'd have used a method that would make it look like a result of his illness – a heart attack or respiratory failure, for example.'

She stops and holds me back by my arm, bringing me to a standstill. She appears to be absolutely delighted and lets me know as much. 'See? That's what I knew I'd be getting with you! That idiot just wanted to get straight in there, whereas if we'd just taken forty-eight hours to prepare we could have done a clean job, no fuss.'

Am I supposed to agree with her? Her enthusiasm is quite childlike, but it's equally contagious. No. I cannot for a single second imagine myself coming up with a plan to execute another human being, but I also have to admit that this young woman has something about her . . . something that gives you the hopeless feeling of wanting to hang on to her every word.

'You do realise,' she continues, 'that if you'd just accepted my proposal from the beginning, we'd be rid of this bastard by now.'

Time to calm things down. Just because I've voiced something that resembles a hypothesis, she's now concluding that I can immediately step into a mercenary's shoes. She's got some imagination. I'm a respected scientist, a responsible man who's never put a foot wrong, and someone whose death is just around the corner. I'm not going to spend the rest of my existence playing around at vigilantism. I want to tell her what I'm thinking but, as always, my words can't follow the same rhythm as my thoughts and I start to stutter. Obviously this is what she was hoping for, because she carries on as if there is nothing wrong.

'OK, we're going to have to be a little patient when it comes to Thule. After even a bungled attempt on his life like this, he's going to be really well protected, and he'd be an idiot to take any pointless risks.

We'll deal with him at a later date. I suggest we turn our attention to the second person on the list.'

And right then, even though we've just set foot on the bustling Rue de Vaugirard, I take the time to make sure nobody can possibly be eavesdropping and hear myself say, 'As you wish. So, who is it?'

I can clearly see that my 'accomplice' is doing her best to disguise her glee, but her efforts are in vain. She positively beams as she speaks. 'You're going to have a field day! I'm pretty sure you must know him . . . and hate him . . . It's Arthur Reimbach.'

CHAPTER 6

In the end, I decide to invite her back to my place. She sits on my sofa in the exact same spot as last time she was here. I put two wine glasses down on the coffee table – I've never owned any champagne flutes – and we wait for the bottle of Roederer Cristal that she bought in the off-licence at the bottom of Rue de Vaugirard to chill in my freezer. Is it possible that I feel even more ridiculous than usual? I'm swinging between two contradictory feelings: pride, because strange as it might seem I'm proud of the decision I've just made; and shame, because I'm not being duped . . . I'm allowing myself to be manoeuvred by Chloé. But as it stands, I'm trying to chase away such thoughts and look at her in a positive light. She's absolutely thrilled, there's no doubt about that, which must be why she bought the bubbly – to seal our pact.

'Should we get down to it?' she asks as she pulls out an identical envelope to the one she gave me last time she was here.

'Sorry?'

'Well, while we're waiting for the champagne, I thought we could look at the best way forward. Do you agree?'

Won over by such determination, I acquiesce, and she passes me a series of photographs on which we can see the plump figure, rounded face and blond wispy hair of this pseudo-journalist who nowadays spends more time attending far-right rallies than penning anything for magazines. Chloé wasn't wrong. I hate him with a visceral passion for his sickening neoreactionary beliefs . . . He's leaving a stunning nineteenth-century apartment building, then crossing the wide pavement before climbing into the back of an enormous Mercedes. He's followed closely by a big bruiser of a bodyguard wearing a suit that's a couple of sizes too small. Another henchman of the same ilk stands a little further back, scrutinising the surrounding area. The last photo is a close-up of the tinted windows of the estate car from behind, through which we can just about make him out.

'I took these photos outside his flat five days ago as he was heading out to record a programme he's going to be on . . .' She pauses and looks at the time on her mobile. 'It's on in about twenty minutes. Do you think we could take a look?'

I respond with a grunt as I remain focused on the photos. I give one back to her. 'Listen . . . Those two men with him . . . Are they . . .'

'They're police officers. A while back there was a group of students who tried to beat him up as he was leaving his publisher's, and now he has full-on protection. This won't make our task any easier, but I'm sure we'll find a solution. Come on.'

She moves along the sofa and pats the place where she's just been sitting, inviting me to get settled. I do as she asks obligingly, and she spreads all the other documents from the envelope out across the table.

'The difficulty,' she says as she picks up a plan of his building, 'is that there's no way we're getting into his place. It's far too well protected. But I can't think of a single other location where we can be certain we'll get our hands on him. He doesn't use an office away from his flat. He's not on any regular radio or TV shows any more. He doesn't write columns for any particular magazine or paper. Basically, he has no fixed schedule we can study in order to work out when we might be able to act.'

I take a closer look at the photos and stop again at the two that show his stocky police bodyguards. I don't want to get on the wrong side of them. Perhaps it's just the air they give off, but everything leads me to believe that the pair of them are the trigger-happy type.

'What about his windows?'

'They overlook an interior garden.'

'Family obligations? Does he have parents or children over on a regular basis?'

'His parents are dead, and he never married. No children he's ever spoken of. We also have a strong suspicion he's gay – maybe even a latent gay, because he's certainly never come out.'

'No hobbies or things he does for himself? I don't know . . . a sport, for example: tennis or a gym membership?'

Chloé roars with laughter at this. It's true that just imagining this fat pig sweating it out on a treadmill is hilarious.

But I remain focused on the task at hand. 'Even though he doesn't have his own show these days, he must appear as a guest pretty often. He's on every channel whenever he brings out a new book or during elections. He gives his opinion even when nobody's asking for it, doesn't he?'

'True enough. But we'd need access to his diary, so we'd know in advance when to act. Not to mention that it's usually the journalists who go to him. He stays put.'

'Hmm . . .'

'What are you thinking?'

'There might be an idea in there somewhere. Why not get ourselves invited over as journalists? We could set up a meeting. Are you sure he lives alone? No staff?'

'Yes, but there's some sort of housekeeper. She's with him a lot, but she doesn't sleep there. She usually works from seven to eleven in the morning and then comes back in the evening from six until nine. Other than that, he's pretty much your typical hermit.'

I hold my head in my hands – not because I want to think more clearly, but because a sudden tiredness has come over me, accompanied by a wave of nausea. I remember now that not three hours ago Professor Lazreg was here giving me my injection and that it was at this exact time last week that I'd started to feel some side effects. I put every effort into pulling myself together so that Chloé sees nothing, and continue to establish my thoughts. Crikey. I'm capable of calculating the trajectory of a microparticle in a cyclotron through numerical integration alone, so I should be able to foresee when and how an overexposed 'political thinker' is going to head out and about around our capital city. I'm interrupted by Chloé, who suddenly jumps up off the sofa.

'Can I go and look in the freezer? I don't want the bottle to explode. It would be such a waste.'

She almost dances as she goes to get the champagne. She returns from the kitchen looking jubilant. This woman is *joie de vivre* personified and yet she's obsessed with killing people. It's quite terrifying, really.

It's a struggle for her to get the cork out – a struggle she doesn't win. I go to her aid and get the job done in a heartbeat.

'To working together!' she cries, lifting her glass.

For a flicker of a moment, I want to say no. I want to say that I won't work with her, that I won't kill anyone . . . and that I won't help her do it either. But the fatigue and desire to vomit remind me that my end is not far from sight. I think back to what Professor Lazreg said. What if he was right? What if there's something I'm supposed to accomplish before I die – something other than the discovery of a new boson with a mass of 126GeV/c2? Something that could be of real use to humankind, or at least the society in which we live . . .

After checking the time on her phone once more, Chloé grabs the remote control, switches the TV on and flicks through the channels.

Arthur Reimbach's face fills the screen. He looks fit to bursting with pride when the presenter mentions that his latest publication, *The Expected Decline*, has sold more than 100,000 copies. He nevertheless does his best to speak with modesty as he explains that this success is in no way due to any literary talent, but simply to people having become aware of the consequences of the mass immigration encouraged by the left, and the mistakes made following May 1968 in terms of the place of women in our society. He describes these as two plagues that will eventually take over our Christian values.

I don't know whether it's what he's saying or the first few sips of the Cristal that make my stomach heave, but I make my apologies to Chloé. 'Sorry about the champagne, but I'm going to have to ask you to leave so I can rest. I really don't feel well at all. My treatment . . .'

'Please don't be sorry! It doesn't matter! We'll make a toast to all this when you're in a better state.'

She is already at the door. When she turns to say her goodbyes, her face shows genuine sympathy; at least, I convince myself it does.

'Promise me you'll take some time to relax. There's no hurry.'

I nod but say nothing. She steps out into the hallway and presses the button for the lift. I wait with her until it arrives, trying to get my thoughts in order and to commit to memory everything we've said to one another this evening. Something strikes me. A detail. Maybe more than that.

'Chloé?'

'Yes?'

'Reimbach's homosexual tendencies – is that just a rumour or can it be verified?'

The lift arrives. She holds the door open, looking like she's deciding whether or not to reveal something to me. 'Are you asking me if I've got actual proof, or are you interested in my personal impressions?'

'Both – if it helps us move forward in any way.'

'It's a rumour. Just a rumour. But, if you want my opinion, I'm convinced he's never been attracted to women. To make the jump from that . . . that he's . . .'

My head is spinning. I understand what she's trying to tell me, but I can't carry on this conversation. 'I'll call you as soon as I'm feeling up to it,' I say, stepping back inside and closing the door behind me.

Tomorrow, I hope.

CHAPTER 7

I fall apart in the minutes following her departure. I go on to have a restless night, shaken by frightening dreams mixed with periods of insomnia during which Reimbach's face looms mockingly in my mind's eye. It must be around five or six in the morning when the worst of the nightmares come. As I lie confused on my bed, his face returns, emaciated this time, a dark shade of grey, and his empty eyes won't leave me.

I go on to get some real sleep just before waking. I feel in much better shape this morning. My appetite is back as I take my usual seat in front of the television, armed with a full cafetière and three slices of brioche smothered in Nutella.

I watch the news, which nearly bores me to death. Football, insipid statements from more or less obscure politicians and reports from seaside resorts where everything is being readied for the season ahead. I have always been able to sit in front of the TV for hours without really watching it, but for the first time in years I turn down the sound to think about the events of the previous day, the commitment I made to Chloé and, above all, what's going to happen next.

What's got into me? Is it Chloé and her charm? The aversion I have towards Arthur Reimbach? Other more obscure reasons linked to my imminent demise? I can't quite fathom how I've got to this point, but one thing stands out, an unavoidable truth: I'm going to kill that piece of filth. At least, I think I'm going to try. All that's left to work out is how . . .

The first essential consideration: this man is under police protection. So there can be no playing at cowboys and just recklessly wading in. I'd stand no chance. Maybe I could make it look like a terrorist attack by planting explosives in his car? No way. I don't want to cause any collateral damage. The only option that seems conceivable to me is to go into his home when we know he's there alone and make a homicide look like a suicide. I mean, why not? That's why I'm interested in his possible homosexuality.

As things stand, I don't think we'd have much chance convincing people that a man like this would kill himself. He's a roaring success. He has never sold so many books, never been as hated by what he calls the bleeding-heart liberals, and never been as in demand by the media. And to their disgrace, he has never been as popular in the eyes of the public. The reactionary element of our society, supported by an ever-increasing number of ordinary citizens, have found a spokesperson to help them appear respectable. It really is high time we intervened and found a believable reason for him to commit suicide.

I wipe my chocolatey fingers on my dressing gown before walking through to my office and turning on my computer. I check through my emails as quickly as I can, resisting the temptation to find out what's been happening with the Large Hadron Collider and the 600 million collisions that happen every second, and get ready for a roam around Google. The first thing I type in is 'Arthur Reimbach rumour'. This search brings up a complaint filed by the man himself against one of the big weeklies for 'publication of malicious rumours'. I then come across a satirical site revealing an affair he is supposed to have had with a rap singer last year. Encouraged by this bit of gossip, I type in 'Is Arthur Reimbach gay?'

I get my money's worth this time. The gay community is clearly making him pay for his stand against equal marriage and he's the butt of a great number of jokes across the main social networks – not all of them in the best taste. I hit upon the idea of clicking on the 'Images' tab in the search engine.

A lot of people have had a lot of fun with Photoshop, it would seem. The more or less crude depictions show the tubby little man in every imaginable position, some requiring extraordinary flexibility, and with all kinds of partners, often endowed with quite astonishing attributes.

Although my brain often has trouble processing humour, I have to admit that these jokes do raise a little chuckle. But this isn't what I came online to find. I need something credible and consistent, something I can start a scandal with – something he won't be able to live down.

OK. Imagine we get past this first hurdle and manage to make his suicide plausible – we're still going to have to stage the entire act so that it raises not a flicker of police suspicion. If we work from the principle that he doesn't take a single step outside unless he's flanked by those two big gorillas, we'll have to, just as I thought yesterday, do the deed at his place.

It's unlikely that he's the type to throw himself off a bridge or under a train anyway. Someone like him would be cowardly. The only method he'd really be capable of would be to take a stomachful of pills. Or maybe he'd open his veins in his bathtub – but even that takes a modicum of courage. So that's sorted. It'll have to be medication and it'll have to be in his flat.

Without even realising it, I'm getting into my stride here. And it's not because of the few extra hours' sleep I managed to get last night. No. Let's be clear about this. It's because Chloé threw down the gauntlet and I've taken it up. This has rarely, if ever, happened to me before; but I'm really on board with it now. So much so that I pick up my mobile to share my intentions with her. I imagine her getting excited. But I get her answerphone. This is the ultimate disappointment.

'*Sorry, Régis. I'm unable to answer. I will call you back as soon as I can.*'

She really did set up a phone line just for me. I feel proud. I'll admit this is childish, but pride is what I'm feeling. I leave her a clumsy message – it's too late to do a complete one-eighty on my nature at this point – and go back to my 'homework'.

Let's have a look at it all logically. Firstly, there's the rumour. I can't use Photoshopped images, as snazzy as they may be. I need something more official. Perhaps a complaint? That's it! It doesn't even matter if it's totally unfounded, as long as it's filed by the police. The most important thing here is that his reputation is sullied enough to make it look like he's been pushed to do the worst. And why would someone press charges against him? Rape? No. Too easy to discredit. Pimping . . . There's definitely more appeal to that. '*Arthur Reimbach organises homosexual orgies . . .*' Yeah, I like that. Now I just need to find someone who'll go to the police. If Chloé really possesses all the means she boasted of when we first met, then she should know how to accomplish it.

And on top of this, we're going to have to act quickly. We can't leave enough time for the scandal to die down or for the police to discover it's a hoax. So, in just a few short days, we'll need to find a way into his place, right under the noses of his bodyguards, and then get out again after having 'suicided' him. All without getting caught. It's pretty complicated if I put it like that, but certainly possible.

My mobile starts ringing just as I'm studying the photos of Reimbach's apartment building. I haven't saved Chloé's number, but I still recognise it . . . or rather, I'm on the lookout for it.

'Hello, Régis. Feeling better?'

She sounds chipper enough, but I also detect a hint of concern which I immediately shrug off.

'Very well. Better, anyway.'

'You tried to get in touch? Sorry – it was a bit difficult.'

'No worries. It was nothing urgent. I just wanted to tell you that I've been starting to think about . . . business. And I wanted to talk to you.'

'Wait! Do you have the envelope I gave you yesterday?'

'Erm, yes . . . I'm actually looking at the photos of . . .'

'There's a SIM card inside. I want you to use it. It'll be more secure. I should have told you about it last night, before I left, but you were too exhausted. Do you have an old mobile phone you could put it in?'

'I don't think so. But I think I can use two different SIMs with this phone. You'll have to give me a bit of time to work out how to do it. I'll get back to you. Does that sound OK?'

I can almost hear her smile at the other end of the line. 'Speak to you later, then.'

It takes me at least half an hour just to open the blasted phone and find the slots for the SIMs. I need a further thirty minutes to track down some instructions online to help me work out how to switch between the two cards. As soon as I feel like I have the system mastered, I call Chloé, as promised.

'Was it really that complicated?' she laughs.

'Don't mock me, please. Give me a Rubik's Cube over one of these devices any day.'

'I didn't know they were still a thing. How long does it take you to solve it, then?'

'Five-point-two-five seconds. I held the record for exactly four months and five days before being beaten by a sixteen-year-old. An American.'

'Are you serious? You were in the Rubik's Cube world championship?'

'Yes. Quite by chance, though. I was at a conference in Holland and the competition was being held in the same hotel. It was a colleague who pushed me into having a go.'

'You'd played it before, though?'

'No. But I'd seen it done and more or less understood what method to apply.'

'Well . . . The most important thing to remember is to call me from this card.'

'Because it's secure?'

'Exactly. It's more than that. There is no possibility of our conversations being listened in on, and no way you can be located through it either. It's in our best interests to be as careful as possible from now on.'

Talking of these basic precautions reminds me of a question that I've been wanting to ask her since our first meeting. As we can't be overheard, I may as well make the most of the opportunity.

'About security . . . You told me that you'd not used your real identity. Can I know your actual name?'

'Don't you like Chloé?'

I'm suddenly swept up by an almost freakish boldness. I try out something that would have been out of the question only seven days earlier. A compliment.

'Yes . . . It really suits you.'

'Let's keep it, then.'

'And Schneider like the actress?'

'She was brilliant. When I was little, I used to dream of being just like her when I grew up. I'm pretty close, wouldn't you say?' She laughs and then adds more seriously, 'At the same time, I'd hate to end up like her. That was a sad little story.' Then she cuts off abruptly and asks, 'Have you found a solution to our problem?'

I can sense her shiver of anticipation as I lay out my battle plan. When I finish, she demonstrates that she has perfectly understood every word. 'That means the first thing we need to do is recruit some little hottie,' she declares, 'who, with gentle financial persuasion, will agree to go to the police and press charges against Reimbach.'

'That's as good a place as any to start.'

'And I have an idea where we might find just the person. I'll pick you up at your place.'

'You're the boss.'

Chapter 8

She's driving a Dacia estate. I'd imagined her in a Fiat 500 or a Mini. Not that I know much about these things, but I'd definitely pictured her in more of what I'd call a 'girly car'. But, no – not this girl. She drives the car of a family on a small budget.

'This isn't yours, is it?' I ask as I walk towards her.

'My what?'

'The car.'

'Yes. Why?'

'It doesn't look like it'd be yours. And because you're in the habit of hiding things from me . . . I assumed you'd have changed your car, too.'

'Poor deduction, my dear Watson! This is indeed my car. But you're right in a way. The plates are false.'

'I wouldn't have expected anything less. So, where are we off to?'

'We're going to a place called "S". It's just "S" – the letter. Do you know it?'

'Should I?'

'If you were into group sex, or had a tendency towards . . . how should I put it? If you were more *voracious*, you might know it.'

I'm tempted to tell her that, even in its most simple forms, sex and I have rarely found common ground, but that my handicaps are already so numerous that I never really think about it. But I don't. I watch the lights through the passenger window and think to myself that this is set to be a night that could trigger all manner of emotions.

◆ ◆ ◆

Even during my worst anxiety attacks, I could never have imagined that such a place existed. They must have gathered everything I hate most about the world and put it under one roof. Starting with crowds. A rapid calculation allows me to ascertain that the total surface area of the establishment is 325 square metres, into which are squashed, at a low estimate, 1,500 people, no doubt of both sexes – but it's difficult to tell them apart given what they're wearing and their outrageous make-up. This is the second time in my entire life that I've set foot in what I would call a disco. I must have been twenty-something when I let myself be dragged along by my CERN colleagues to some place just like this. I remember it being a particularly trying experience. What I recall most vividly are the thick clouds of sickening nicotine and the overpowering stench of armpits. While I'd be at a loss to tell you what music was being played, I'm sure of one thing – it was nothing like the noises attacking my eardrums tonight. Add to this all the alcohol and stink of sweat and I can sense that my career as a killer will soon have to be aborted if coming to this hellhole is going to be a regular occurrence. Chloé saves me by taking my hand and leading me to the far end of the room to get a drink.

There are two of them working behind the bar. A boy and a girl. Both of them are dressed in ripped vests and kilts.

'What are you having?' Chloé howls at me while trying to attract their attention.

'A beer if they have them.'

'Of course they have them. Don't start playing up, Régis.'

The young barmaid finally notices the frantic waves of my friend and asks us what we want to drink through a series of gestures alone.

When she arrives with two halves, Chloé leans over the bar to make herself heard. I don't catch a single word of their conversation, but I guess she's asked the girl if she can speak to the male bartender because she goes to fetch him, and we watch as he walks towards us with a far from pleasant look on his face.

'What do you want?' he asks, his face averted as if he can't look us in the eye.

His profile reveals him to be a lot older than I'd first thought. His features are prominent and one might guess that behind all the make-up, which I find odd for a man in the first place, lies a countenance that has seen a little too much in this life.

'Hi there, Karl. My name's Chloé. They must have told you I was coming in tonight.'

This 'they' that she mentions must have some sort of influence on the barman, because he deigns to look at us now and flashes what we could, with a little optimism, take to be a smile.

'That's right. Come with me.'

We follow him like well-behaved little children as he leads the way through what feels like herds of wild animals to a spiral staircase. We climb up to a gallery overlooking the dance floor where a handful of revellers, probably off their heads on booze or worse, are hanging over the railings or sitting slumped in red velvet armchairs. We are above the speakers now and the noise level is a smidgen more tolerable. Karl positions himself at a safe distance from the drunks and leans on the railing.

'OK! So, you're looking for a docile type of escort. Someone not too fussy about the type of client they'll work with. Have I got that right?'

'Yes. You could put it like that. What we really need is . . .'

'Tut, tut! I don't want to know what you're going to be doing with him. All I've been asked to do is to show you who' – he points down towards the mass of people on the dance floor – 'might need the money enough to accept something a little out of the ordinary. That's as far as I want to get involved.'

'We realise that. We're listening.'

He doesn't take long to find what he's looking for. He points out a young Arab man, a very effeminate type who, we learn, goes by the name of Luigi. We watch him as he dances.

'He'd fuck just about anything if it meant he could make the money he needs for his surgery in the States. He's easy-going enough, but I don't think you can ask him to go too far.'

His eyes continue to search the crowd. He then indicates a big guy, tattooed from top to toe.

'Anton! He'll do anything you ask. Nothing puts him off. But you need to watch it . . . He's a complete dope fiend and he's already got a name for himself with the police. So you might question his reliability, you know what I mean?'

I nod along with Chloé as if I actually know what he's talking about.

Just like a salesman in an electrical goods store, he moves on to the next item and proposes Marvin, a young man dressed rather more conservatively than the other patrons. A stray strand of hair falls over his eyes and he boasts a piercing on his top lip. There's nothing that would differentiate him from your typical teenager.

'As for him . . . I don't really know what to tell you. He hasn't been working here all that long, but I know he needs to get his hands on some cash. I don't know how far he'd be prepared to go to get it, but according to his clients he's all right.'

Karl evidently considers his inventory complete, because he turns to us and addresses Chloé. Only Chloé.

'I'll let you sort it out with them. If you need my help again, you can count on it, but make sure you're not in here every night, please. See ya!'

We watch as he saunters past what looks like an addict struggling to catch his breath in one of the chairs and runs back down the stairs, to the relief of his clearly overwhelmed colleague behind the bar.

'An interesting character,' I say to Chloé. 'Do you know a lot of people like him?'

'None. He's a friend of some friends . . . friends I don't even know that well, but who do come in useful from time to time. There's the proof. So, what do you think?'

'I think we should be able to make a quick enough decision, don't you? Reimbach has often expressed his aversion to Arabs and Muslims, so we can exclude the first one straight away. I didn't really understand what the deal was with the second guy, but I didn't get a good feeling about him . . .'

'There's no way we can get mixed up with someone who's already been involved with the police. He's out of the running, I agree.'

'So that leaves us with Marvin.'

'We need to get a move on.'

We hurry back down into the bear pit. As we're heading to Marvin's table, a tall and busty blonde starts to paw at Chloé's buttocks. She takes it better than I might have expected and simply removes the woman's hand before continuing on her way. At the same time, I give a somewhat confused smile in response to a man with a moustache and leather baseball cap who asks if I'd like to join him and his friends for a drink.

Although the clientele are clearly intent on including us in their fantasies, I'm not convinced that we're fully blending in here. Quite the opposite, I would imagine. On top of this, the young man is very much on the defensive as soon as Chloé makes it clear that we want to talk to him.

'Hello, Marvin. Let me introduce myself. Chloé Schneider. And this is my friend Régis.'

'Yeah?'

I wouldn't say his response is aggressive, but he gives a hint of a sneer.

'Could we get you a drink? We'd like to chat with you a while,' Chloé continues.

'You can get me a drink. And we can talk. But I don't really want it to last a "while". I'd like to be able to get some work done tonight.'

'Well, that's what this is about.'

'You? You two? Work with you two? That's a joke, right?'

'Not at all. Though it may not be the sort of work you're used to. But come and listen.'

The young man hesitates for a moment and looks like he's wondering whether following a pair like us is the right thing to do. He even holds on to his chin while he decides. 'What about this one? Does he ever open his mouth?'

Chloé laughs loudly as she stares at me. Fair enough, compared with her I feel like a bit of an oddball – but there's no need for her to rub it in.

'Sure. He speaks sometimes, but what he says is not always intelligible and not always all that interesting. Come on, it'll only take us fifteen minutes to tell you what we want, and you can make up your mind afterwards.'

Won over by Chloé's charisma, Marvin takes us up on our offer and we all go to get refills. I try to stride with confidence in the hope that I'll go unnoticed on the dance floor. This is pointless. As well as the general vulgarities thrown my way, I have to contend with more than one pair of adventurous hands. Quite the gauntlet.

When we reach the bar, Chloé turns to ask the young man what he'd like, then puts me in charge of getting in a mojito for him and another beer each for us. I decline yet another invitation – even more outrageous than the offers I've had so far – as we make our way back up to the gallery, where we can pursue our conversation in a slightly quieter environment.

As I put the three glasses down on the table, I note that it's made from transparent fibreglass laid on a casting of a copulating couple. Tasteful.

Chloé is doing her best to strike a chord with young Marvin. 'Let me be totally clear with you,' she declares. 'I couldn't give a toss how you earn your living. You must have your reasons.'

'You've got that right, yes.'

'But if those reasons are purely financial, we can help you earn a lot more . . . and in a lot less time. Are you interested?'

'Just cut the crap and get to the point.'

'I'm getting there. Just answer me this: are you in this profession as a career move, or are you just out to make as much as you can as quickly as possible?'

The young buck looks on the verge of fleeing, but still appears to want to know more. Strangely, he turns to me to help him make up his mind. I try to give him a reassuring smile. Miracle of miracles – it works.

'I need megabucks,' he splutters. 'And I need it fast.'

'Very good,' replies Chloé, clearly pleased with this admission. 'You don't have to give me all the ins and outs, but I do need to know whether it's to clear some sort of . . . dodgy . . . debt. The sort of debt that might involve gambling or drugs.'

'It's nothing like that. I'm totally clean. And I've got nothing to hide either. I just need to get out of here. I want to move over to Australia, where I have a friend . . . and I need some funds, so I don't have to show up there like a beggar.'

'And how much are we talking?'

He turns to me again as if checking whether or not he should answer. I don't get the chance to give him any signs of approval this time because Chloé pipes up again.

'Come on. Give me a number.'

He hesitates for a further few seconds, looking sidelong at this woman who's come from nowhere as if she's Mother Christmas, before answering in a timid tone, 'Twenty grand?'

'We'll give you thirty if you accept our offer tonight and promise to make your way down under as soon as the job is finished. That means within a fortnight, three weeks tops.'

It's not only the young gigolo who's left breathless at the sum. I remember Chloé talking of financial means and if she isn't bluffing, she can get the drinks in from now on.

Marvin takes his time digesting the news. I'm certain he must already be imagining himself out in the Pacific, lying on a beach surrounded by blond, bronzed surfer types. But whatever his motivations might be, he isn't backward in coming forward.

'What do I have to do?'

'Arthur Reimbach. Do you know him?'

Chapter 9

The effects are devastating. Lodged at the beginning of the week, precisely when the newspapers don't have much in the way of news, Marvin's complaint is initially published by *Le Canard enchaîné* before the rest of the papers follow suit. Some report it in a sober fashion whereas others, particularly the left-leaning press, have a field day. Ten days later, via an opinion piece on TV, it all reaches a climax. Just as one might expect, Reimbach, in turn, presses charges for defamation of character. Marvin makes an indirect reply to him by agreeing to a TV interview in which he reveals in extensive detail how he was made the sexual plaything of the well-known patriot and two of his friends at night-time orgies held in Reimbach's apartment.

It is only following this interview that our target starts to adopt the attitude we want from him. He's done with crying slander and conspiracy. Little by little, he shies away from all journalists, saying that justice will prevail and that this case has already caused enough harm to his family and loved ones.

While all this is going on, Chloé and I aren't simply biding our time. We keep in regular contact with Marvin and coach him as to how to handle the press – even getting him to tone it down on occasion. Along with the entire gay community, he hates Reimbach and is obviously taking great pleasure in dragging him through the mud. But he could so easily get carried away. We have to keep an eye on it. Above all, we do not let our future victim out of our sights. We take turns to follow him everywhere he goes, and we meet regularly to exchange any information we collect during these long hours in the field.

We have planned to have lunch today. It's almost one o'clock when I collapse into a booth in a large brasserie in the Les Halles district. I'm actually doing a little better than I was earlier today. I saw Lazreg just twenty-four hours ago and his awful treatment means I should really be resting. It's been a long morning. I've felt sick, but more than that . . . I've felt down. For the first time since receiving my death sentence, I feel a definite anxiety and even sadness. I feel that in losing this life – a life I've found until now to be insipid and undesirable in every sense – I'll lose feelings that I've never known before, and which are only just being offered to me now. And it's all too late.

I'm not a fool and I'm not trying to hide from the truth. I know it's Chloé who has brought me all this.

She fascinates me.

Nothing gets the better of her. Nothing scares her. She charges through her existence with relentless enthusiasm. As head of a humanitarian organisation, she'd surely be able to put an end to world hunger or reduce global warming by a couple of degrees. But no. She's decided to dedicate part of her life to killing people. And why not?

Oh! I almost forgot an important little detail. I tried my luck.

That's right. I, Régis Gaudin, dared to believe that I could have a sexual relationship (unpaid for) with a woman. And not just any woman, but the woman who had all the girls down at S eating out of her hand, no less.

She turned me down, obviously. But she was kind about it and didn't say anything that would hurt my feelings. I even feel like her 'no' could well have been a 'yes' if I'd chosen another moment or gone about it in a different way . . . or had more confidence in myself. If she had accepted, she'd have been the fifth woman I've ever known – in the biblical sense. I'm not exactly departing this life with a lot of notches on my bedpost, am I?

Women are just so complicated. Compared with the female of the species, the Fermi-Dirac integral or Pauli's exclusion principle are child's play.

Here she is now. She looks beautiful – as always. She glows – as always. And she looks particularly elegant in her flimsy little dress. My lustful thoughts disappear as quickly as they enter my head, because as she sits opposite me there's not the slightest tenderness in her demeanour. She's attentive, but no more than that.

'How do you feel now? You didn't look too great this morning.'

'I wasn't. I've been in quite a bit of pain, but it's improved over the last couple of hours or so. What are you having?'

'Got your appetite back?'

'Yes. I'm a little hungry, in fact.'

'A seafood platter and champagne? How does that sound?'

'Are we celebrating something?'

'Yes!'

Minutes later, I gaze at her eyes shining through the bubbles in her champagne flute. She invites me to clink glasses, and I grumble a little as I sip the Moët & Chandon. It's cold, dry and fizzy. And that's all I can say about it. Give me beer any day of the week. Perhaps this is some other odd and anarchic way in which my brain works. I have no idea when it comes to taste. I couldn't tell a table wine from a classified *grand cru*. But it saves me money. I'm quite down-market when it comes to alcohol. But this isn't the case with Chloé, who, it seems, will use just about any pretext to open a bottle of the sparkly stuff.

'Do you actually like it?' I ask.

It's impossible for her to have followed my train of thought and she needs clarification.

'What, the champagne?'

'Yes.'

'I love it! Nothing gives me more pleasure.'

She replies with a spontaneity I've come to expect from her, but an expressionless look falls across her face within seconds. She looks so very serious, ashen – as though I've awakened a painful memory.

'What's going on? Have I said something I shouldn't?'

'Not at all. I was just . . . thinking of you.'

'Ah! A pleasant thought indeed! You look delighted!' I flash her a grin.

She bats away my remark. 'Don't be silly.' She seems almost embarrassed, or confused. She continues. 'Actually, it *is* your fault.'

'What did I do?'

'Nothing. It's just that you make me feel guilty. I really enjoy myself when we're together and I think about the adventure we're about to embark on . . . but I just wish I could do something for you. I want to make you happy, and I feel as though I just have to put all that to one side every time we meet.' She stops, and takes a little time to think before speaking again. 'And I'm sorry about the way I spoke to you when you asked me . . . You know what I mean.'

'It's no problem.'

'I hope I wasn't too harsh? It's not easy for me . . . that kind of thing. I was hurt badly . . . and since then . . .'

I don't want to hear anything about her romantic history and I have even less desire to listen to her justify herself. The last thing I want is her sleeping with me out of pity. My dismal career as a seducer hasn't seen a major event now for over three years. It's a fiasco.

I wave my hand at her, giving her permission to stop talking. 'Forget all that. Tell me what's happening with Reimbach instead.'

She seems relieved, and is clearly eager to change the subject. 'We're serving him up on a platter.'

'What's been going on?'

'It looks as though he's really fallen into a deep depression. His doctor has been to see him. As soon as he left, that housekeeper woman went straight to the chemist. I followed her, and I overheard what he'd been prescribed – antidepressants. And they're going to have to be injected. Do you get me?'

'Yes! We can pretend to be nurses.'

'Bingo! All we have to do is get in there before the real nurse, and then he or she will discover the body. Suicide by overdose.'

It's now or never. I think about how we're going to implement all this. Will we have to forestall the nurse? It seems a little risky. It'd be better to simply replace her altogether; then we'd know she wasn't going to show up. We could telephone the district nurse's office and cancel the appointment. That would leave us enough time to complete our operation. I tell Chloé what I'm thinking and although she agrees, she does put a dampener on it.

'It's a great idea, but there are a couple of other things I need to tell you. One's good news, and the other is . . . well, we'll see. Should I start with the good news?'

'Go ahead.'

'The housekeeper asked the chemist for the number of a nurse. He gave her a specific name and telephone number. She said she needed one to come over in the afternoon just after lunch. I didn't catch the whole number, but I do have the name, so it should be easy enough to find. And the other piece of news is . . .'

'I'm listening.'

'The nurse's name is Thomas Guinard. So . . .'

'It's going to have to be me.'

She watches my face for signs of apprehension. I reassure her. What she's told me doesn't bother me in the least. It's as if I've already accepted the idea of becoming a killer. This is what she wants from me anyway.

I've never really been that fond of humans and one I particularly hate is coming within reach; so that will make it all a little easier, won't it? I consent with a nod – albeit a slightly restrained one – adding that I hope I'm up to it. Chloé confirms that she doesn't doubt it for a second as the waiter in his immaculate white shirt and long black apron comes to refill our glasses. Cheers!

CHAPTER 10

'Be serious, Régis! We're never going to manage it.'

She's funny. First there was the hair dye. Forty-five minutes of a foul-smelling liquid on my head and having to put up with her dubious jokes on the resulting younger looks it would bring me. Then the rubber prosthesis on my cheeks and jawline, and now blue contact lenses. I've always hated being touched, anywhere at all – but my *eyes*! Every time Chloé nears me with those wretched lenses, I close my eyes tightly. I just can't help it. She asks me to look up at the ceiling, but that doesn't work. And when I look down . . . I just get an eyeful of her cleavage and that doesn't help matters either.

I can sense that she's starting to get annoyed with me. 'Do you think you could follow my instructions if I put a polo neck on?'

She noticed, then. This isn't easy. I'm exacerbating the situation. I need to get a grip and let her get on with it. She wrestles with me, pushes my head backwards, and there it is . . . The first one is in place. It wasn't that bad, as it turns out. I'm less apprehensive when it comes to the second, and thirty seconds later I'm all done. I have become (according to Chloé, who very rarely spares my feelings) 'tall, dark and handsome with stunning blue eyes'.

'You're unrecognisable,' she tells me.

I want to verify this for myself and go straight to my bathroom. I slip on the regulation white trousers, Crocs and pale-blue tunic of a nurse before taking a look at what we've created. The image in the mirror frightens me, but it's very convincing. I look, as she said, nothing like myself. So much so that if I stepped outside and bumped into a neighbour, I know they wouldn't recognise me. Not a single one of them would make the link between the man I now see in front of me and the 'autistic chap on the third floor'. I'm feeling confident about what's next and go back to join Chloé in the living room.

'All good? Ready to go?' I ask her, picking up the medical bag we put together earlier.

'Wait! You're forgetting something important.'

I hesitate for a moment because I can't think of a single thing we might have forgotten – other than photo ID and a nursing degree, neither of which I could obtain at such short notice.

'Such as?'

'Intravenous administration,' she replies.

'Intravenous administration. Yes. What about it?'

'You're going to have to practise. I'm sure you have absolutely no idea how to give someone an intravenous injection.'

'Don't worry about it.'

'I'm serious, Régis.'

'So who am I supposed to practise on? You?'

'Obviously you can't go as far as actually injecting me, but at least do a tourniquet or something and prepare the syringe.'

I open up the bag, remove a rubber band and tie it around the top of Chloé's arm. I take a piece of cotton wool and soak it in a little alcohol before rubbing it over her most prominent vein. Then I pick up the syringe I've already placed on the table and push the piston as if removing the air bubbles. I am now ready to inject. I look my patient straight in the eye.

'Well?'

There is definitely a hint of admiration in her eyes. 'It looks like you've been doing it forever. I bet it was your profession in a past life!'

'No, but I can't tell you the number of injections and blood tests I've had over the past year. It's given me plenty of opportunities to watch nurses work.'

This reminder of exactly what I've had to cope with since first being diagnosed makes her visibly uncomfortable. I pack up my equipment, then get to my feet.

'Shall we go?'

Without a word, she stands to follow me. And then we're off.

◆ ◆ ◆

'Just a second, please.'

The policeman on the door couldn't look more like a member of his profession if he tried. He is bulky, somewhere in his fifties and has a full head of dark hair and thick eyebrows. He is wearing a suit which barely hides the revolver holstered under his left armpit.

He holds up one hand as he presses the intercom with the other. The voice that comes through is muffled, like something at a fast-food drive-in. I'm unable to tell whether it belongs to a man or a woman. I hear the police officer say that the nurse has arrived (thank you, officer!) and I assume he's given the go-ahead because he opens the door and beckons me through, pointing towards the entrance hall beyond a pair of glass doors.

I'm just about to make my way towards the stairs at the end of the hallway when the officer stops me and asks to look in my bag. He doesn't take long examining the few syringes, bandages and boxes of pills before giving me a quick pat-down.

I feel numb. I simply ready myself for what lies ahead. I know that we've done everything we can and not left much to chance. Everything will go as planned. All I have to do is keep telling myself that in just a few minutes I'm going to kill a man. Either the thought is too abstract or I've discovered my true vocation in life, because this truth has no effect on my behaviour whatsoever.

When he gives me the all-clear, I walk through the second set of doors.

As expected, when I reach Reimbach's floor the housekeeper opens the door to me. She is the image of the values her employer so often preaches: straight-backed, stiff and severe-looking. She looks like she's just left mass. And that the mass was in Latin.

I introduce myself as Thomas Guinard as she examines me from head to toe before inviting me to enter. I follow her through the apartment, noting the plush but old-fashioned furnishings and ornaments. Opposite a heavy double door opening into one of the living rooms, she leads me down a long corridor, at the end of which she moves to one side, allowing me to step into a large bedroom. There he is, lying on the bed in a red velvet dressing gown. Without even knowing it, he is adding such drama to his imminent demise. He turns to me, the harrowed look of a beaten dog on his face – but there is still something belittling in the way he looks at me.

I don't think it necessary to say hello and turn back to address the housekeeper instead. 'Do you have the medication?'

'It's in the fridge. The chemist told me to keep it cool. I'll go and get it for you.'

'Thank you.'

I walk over to him and open up my bag, pulling out a single-use syringe. My movements are calm and measured. If I feel the slightest emotion, it's an almost imperceptible rise in adrenalin which is stimulating me just enough to get the job done. As we wait for the housekeeper to come back from the kitchen, I get out my bottle of rubbing alcohol and open up a fresh packet of cotton balls. Reimbach is already busy rolling up the sleeve of his gown.

I repeat the same steps I performed earlier in front of Chloé. I'm just finishing up when the housekeeper arrives with the drugs. I take them from her and she has the wise idea of leaving us to it.

As I fill up the syringe, I question him. 'Have you been prescribed anything else?'

He doesn't give me a response, but instead opens up the drawer of his bedside cabinet and pulls out two packets of tablets. I use these three seconds of diversion to throw what I've just prepared into the bottom of my bag and swap it with the pre-filled syringe of Chloé-concocted cocktail. When he turns back towards me, I take the tablets from him and examine them with the air of a concerned medical professional.

'When did you last take these?'

'Lunchtime,' he replies, breathing a sigh of exasperation.

'After the injection, I don't want you to take any more until tomorrow morning.'

He returns them to the drawer and nods slowly as he stretches out his arm again. I feel like he can't wait for this to be over and done with. The same goes for me. I place the needle into his vein and press down on the plunger. A pearly drop of blood runs out of the hole I've just made. Reimbach doesn't take his eyes off me. I believe, in this instant, that he's guessed what I'm doing to him. But it would seem not. He doesn't recoil or struggle. He lets me put the substance into his body –a liquid that will put him to sleep for longer than he thinks.

The effects are almost instant. Within a few seconds he starts to look lethargic . . . but agitated. His eyes appear to plead with me. He really does know now. He knows that something unexpected is happening. I only have a few seconds left. I hastily pull out the needle, slip on a pair of latex gloves, open the drawer of the bedside cabinet and empty the two packets of tablets. With one hand I pull down his jaw, and with the other I shove the tablets into the back of his mouth. He tries to push me away. He tries to spit them back out. But he's too weak to fight me and his natural reflex takes over. His swallowing reflex.

He's coming to an end. Inevitably, the autopsy will conclude that his death was due to a drug overdose. I'm just about to remove the gloves when I spot a laptop on a sideboard. I walk over to it and hit a key at random. It flickers on and the screen lights up. There's no request for a password. I open up Google and look at his 'Favourites' tab. Twitter's up there. I know he is (or was) very active on social media. His session opens up automatically. This is just too good. Thoughts are whizzing through my mind. I make every effort to emulate his style and type as quietly as I can.

> *I tried to let you all know what was coming. In return, I became the target of those who wish to put an end to our culture and values. With no regrets, I'm happy to say – sort it out yourselves!*

I leave the laptop open and take off my gloves as I walk back to the bed. I lean in to take a closer look at Reimbach. He's fallen back on to the pillows and is moving his head from left to right in slow motion. A thin trail of saliva falls from his lips. He's unable to control his movements and I doubt very much he can articulate a single word at this point. I gather together my belongings and leave the room. There's no need for me to look at him again.

The housekeeper is in the living room waiting for me. Her face shows concern. Something tells me she must be really attached to Reimbach.

'Is he OK?'

'His doctor prescribed a very powerful sedative. He was just nodding off as I left the room. If you want to go and check on him, I'd do it now if I were you. He'll be fast asleep any minute.'

I watch as she walks back to the room and pokes her head through the door. She takes a glance before closing it quietly.

'I think it's best if I let him rest,' she says as she comes back to me. 'Let me show you out.'

At the front door to the apartment, I politely shake the hand of this devoted woman, advising her to ensure that her boss doesn't exceed the prescribed doses. Then I walk unhurriedly down the stairs. I play over the last few minutes in my head and convince myself that the reason I'm totally devoid of emotion must be that I didn't actually see him die. Because he just fell asleep.

Chapter 11

As predicted, the autopsy reveals a massive overdose and my fake tweet is taken at face value. For three full days, his 'suicide' causes a huge stir, and it's enough to mislead the investigators. I get a few twinges of guilt when I find out about them interrogating poor Thomas Guinard, but he's only in custody for five hours and he leaves the police station with a story to dine off for years to come.

To avoid a media circus, the prosecutor decides not to reveal immediately that a criminal investigation is underway. This suits us perfectly, even though the photofit of the presumed killer is so far removed from my actual sorry appearance that I feel safe from suspicion.

So we're not worried in the slightest, and on Chloé's initiative – and because we want to celebrate this first success – we go on a short break for a few days. My first ever holiday, if we don't include camping trips my parents sent me on as a teenager (on which I just got bullied for the duration by the other boys and had to be sent home early). Yes: Chloé manages to get me to agree to what would have been impossible only three weeks earlier – a genuine holiday.

She doesn't manage to bring about a total transformation in me, though. I still refuse to get on a plane. But after umpteen discussions on the subject in which she employs a full charm offensive, I give in and we agree to go on a spa break in Quiberon.

I make her laugh when I frown like an undergraduate tackling the Schrödinger equation whenever a masseuse comes anywhere near me (or whenever I simply suspect a masseuse might be thinking about coming near me). She gives up champagne temporarily and replaces it with the local cider. But the Breton climate at this time of year – twenty minutes of blue sky for every four hours of rain – encourages me to return to my old self. So the trip isn't as successful as all that.

During this time away, we make an agreement to not bring up the Reimbach affair nor speak of any possible future operations until we return to Paris.

So, having left all the cider and galettes behind, we find ourselves back at my place early one evening to mull over what will happen next, accompanied by beer and crisps.

'Soon back to old habits,' she says to me, almost reproachfully.

'People can't change their natures.'

'What about my waistline? Have you given that any thought?'

'Well, if you start piling it on, we'll just have to go back to the spa, won't we?'

'Unbelievable! You liked it that much you're ready to go back? Hard to believe, seeing as you had a shit fit every time one of those massage girls tried to lay a finger on you.'

'Erm . . . that's a bit of an exaggeration. Let's just say that I know what holidays are all about now . . . and they're not all that unpleasant. That probably has something to do with the fact that I went with you, though. The spa bit should be optional.'

'Fair enough. But getting away seems to have recharged your batteries anyway. Did you notice just now that you gave me a compliment – a real one – without stammering or saying anything weird?'

'Wow. I've become a real man, then.'

'Hmm . . .'

She grabs a big handful of crisps and swallows them down along with half her beer before throwing an almost challenging look in my direction. 'Shall we get down to it, then?'

'You're the boss.'

It's the second time I've called her this and, even though she rolls her eyes, I know she loves it. I can tell.

'Right! Let's go!'

I have trouble taking my eyes off the new envelope she's just put down on the table. It looks exactly the same as the last one. Chloé looks pleased with herself as she picks it up and opens it. Her eyes change colour and become a lighter blue. I've noticed that this happens whenever she's excited or anticipating something. She pulls out a series of photos and proceeds to spread them out in front of us. They're of a plumpish brunette in her forties. Some of them are close-ups, others are full-length. She's not what I'd call smart. She's dressed down in either a shirt and jeans or black trousers and a dark sweater. But something does strike me. She's grinning in every picture. In fact, I believe she's actually laughing in one of them. This same *joie de vivre* is evident in every single snap.

'Stéphanie Tisserand,' declares Chloé. 'Ring a bell?'

'Nothing. Absolutely no idea.'

'That's fine. This woman is second to none when it comes to discretion. Even though . . .'

'Yeah?'

'She's the head of a massive human trafficking operation between France and Eastern Europe.'

'What? Her?'

'Yes. And as you can gather from these pics, I don't think what she does stops her sleeping at night. But it's estimated that she brings hundreds of girls a year into the country, minors more often than not, who, depending on their "qualities", find themselves in the exclusive service of some wealthy old pervert or in a luxury brothel at best. Sometimes . . .

a few of them have ended up chopped up in an abandoned van under the ring road. Nice, right?'

I examine the photographs more closely now. How is this even possible? Not her line of work – because we know that it exists already – but that it's a woman running the show? It's inconceivable, really. Especially this woman I'm looking at right now. She seems so bubbly and bright.

My face must show my scepticism because Chloé adds, 'We needed some time to get all our proof together. She's extremely careful. I've never come across anyone like her. But we have no doubt. We need to act soon.'

I don't say a word. I bite my bottom lip and push the photos over to the far side of my coffee table, just keeping one of them in my grip.

Chloé must be imagining what's running through my head. 'I know what you're thinking, Régis. That it's a woman and that you—'

'You don't miss a thing, do you?' I interrupt her because the point she's making seems pretty self-evident to me.

'You think that from a moral point of view this will be more complicated. That's it, isn't it?'

'Well, it's understandable, isn't it?'

'You're wrong. As soon as you get anywhere near her, you'll know it's the right thing to do. Trust me. Now – do you want me to brief you or not?'

I'm not feeling fully convinced as I glance down at my watch. We have half an hour before Professor Lazreg's visit.

'Go ahead. But you know I'm waiting for my doctor, don't you? We'll have to break for a few minutes and I can't have him seeing any of this stuff. He might start wondering what it is.' I point to the photos of our future victim.

Chloé picks them up and stuffs them back into the envelope.

'I completely forgot,' she says apologetically. 'I'll go now. I know that you don't usually feel all that good after your treatment.'

'No! Please don't leave!'

Chloé raises her eyebrows in surprise. I'm sure she's thinking that, after those few days away and my awful attempts at chatting her up, I'm becoming too pushy.

I try to reassure her. 'The side effects don't kick in for a few hours,' I remind her.

'Régis! Do I have to spell this out again? What we're up to here isn't exactly what you'd call legal, is it? If we run into a problem down the line, I'd really rather nobody you know had seen us together.'

'He won't see you. You can stay in here and I'll take him to my room and then show him straight back out of the door. Plus, I have to admit that I've been finding him a little on the intrusive side anyway. He's a kind man, but he hangs around trying to get me to open up and share my feelings. He's always wanting to chat about how I'm dealing with my death sentence. If I tell him I have company, I don't think he'll dare stick around. Please stay.'

I'm not sure she's overly enthralled by my proposition because she lets out a heavy sigh and says, 'If you want.'

It sounds false. But as soon as we resume our earlier conversation, she appears to forget all about being annoyed. 'The first thing you need to know is that she works under the umbrella of an official company – events management. And she's the director. What she says she does is supply hostesses for conferences and exhibitions and the like. She has some major international companies on her books as well as top civil servants. Her reputation is up there with the best of them. From the outside, it looks like she just goes about her life as your typical career woman. She lives in the sixteenth arrondissement, just opposite the Auteuil racing track, and her offices are in Neuilly. She travels there by car every morning and tends to spend most of her day there. Every now and again she might venture out to see a client or go to one of the exhibitions to check on her girls. But it's all just a front.' She's just about to grab another handful of crisps but changes her mind and pushes the dish towards me. 'Get these away from me, will you? I'll end up exploding.'

'Shall I get you another beer, then, to wash them down?'

'Erm . . . Go on, then . . . Just one more.'

I leave for a minute or so to fetch another couple of 1664s. When I get back to her, Chloé is whispering into her mobile phone – not the one she uses for our conversations, but the other one. I turn around to leave the room and give her some space, but she calls me back.

'It's OK, Régis. I'm done. I just had to leave a message for a friend.'

Obediently (as has been the case since I first started getting to know her), I sit back down and open our beers. Again, she downs half the bottle in a couple of swigs, with a pleasure that shows how quickly she's forgotten her reticence.

'Back to the dark side,' she says, wiping her mouth on her sleeve. 'First things first – during the week, she drives herself to her office in her own car. But if she's ever conducting business – the bits of it that we're interested in – she's escorted by at least one bodyguard. They change all the time, so it's difficult to keep track. According to our information, it would seem that they're all members of her Eastern European network and that their visits to France don't last more than a couple of weeks. Something else you need to know: she herself is always armed when she's out and about with her girls. A handgun – a 9mm Glock. It's discreet, but effective.'

'This is like something out of one of those dark Scandinavian TV series,' I remark.

'You haven't heard the half of it. I'd say that most of her clients for the girls she'd refer to as her "elite merchandise" are massive drug and arms dealers. And these girls are just lambs to the slaughter. It's the Albanian mafia that takes them, mainly. You can imagine . . . We're dealing with the crème de la crème of organised crime here.'

'Yes . . . She sounds charming. But there is something I'd like to—'

I'm interrupted by the sound of the doorbell. My dear doctor has turned up with his magic potions, which means I have a few difficult hours ahead of me.

When I open the door, he flashes the caring smile I've come to know so well, but there's something a little more harried than usual about him. My impression is confirmed when he starts making apologies the second he's inside.

'I'm so sorry, but I'm in a terrible rush. I need to be out of your hair as soon as possible tonight.'

He starts to make his way towards the living room, which is where he usually tortures me, but I tap him on the arm and point instead along the corridor.

'My apologies, but I have company tonight. Is it all right with you if we do this in my bedroom?'

'What? Oh . . . Yes, of course.'

I pop my head around the living room door and assure Chloé that I'll only be a few minutes before leading the doctor to my room and sitting down on the bed. As he takes out his stethoscope and blood pressure monitor, he asks, almost absent-mindedly, 'So, how have things been this week?'

My need to gather my thoughts forces me to delay a little and I don't give him an immediate response. But wasn't he the one who wanted me to find something adventurous to do before I die? What would he think of me if he knew? Régis Gaudin is not just a ridiculous stick-in-the-mud incapable of the slightest change to his boring little life after all.

'I've had a very good week. I went to Brittany for a few days.'

There it is. He stares at me. It looks like I've pressed the pause button on old Lazreg. His eyes widen as if checking to see if it's actually me who's speaking. He shakes his head a little, bringing himself back to reality, and manages to whisper, 'Well . . . that's good. That's very, very good, in fact.'

He straps the blood pressure monitor on to my arm and starts to inflate it. This is the worst bit. I feel like he won't stop pumping until every vein in my body has burst. Then he tells me it says 120 over 60, which isn't too bad at all. He frowns a little and mutters something that I'm unable to quite catch.

'Is something wrong, Doctor?'

It's plain how preoccupied he is, because as he turns to me it's almost as if he's surprised to see me there. 'What? No . . . It's just that you seem to be handling the treatment fairly well. I think you're in better shape than you were last week, wouldn't you say? Perhaps it was your little holiday?'

He forces out a laugh and I don't really like it. I mean, it's not as if he can really tell how far my disease has spread (or not) just by taking my blood pressure. He looks a little less nervous as he readies the syringe. I'm getting a sudden Dr Frankenstein vibe from our eminent Professor Lazreg. How am I going to get him to open up?

I try a little humour. 'Do you think I might be cured? Is that it?'

As I imagined, he smiles apologetically at my weak attempt at a joke and replies frankly. 'Not at all, unfortunately. But you knew that already, didn't you?'

I nod, but make no reply.

'I was actually thinking about something else,' he continues, 'and I think I'm going to have to make a confession.'

This gets my attention all right. Might he have lied to me about how ill I am? Is the end even nearer than we thought? I surprise myself with how anxious I feel, and he must read the worry in my eyes because his voice is calm and reassuring as he explains himself.

'Please don't be too concerned. It's nothing more serious than what you're already dealing with. Only . . .'

He pauses as he presses the needle into my arm. I watch him and think about the injection I gave Reimbach. He doesn't seem any surer of himself than I did. In fact, I actually think I might have made a better job of it.

When he finishes, he points to the syringe and his demeanour becomes solemn all of a sudden.

'You were saying?' I prompt him.

'As I explained, this treatment hasn't been put on the market yet and the reason I have to do the injections myself is because I can't ask anyone else to administer them.'

'I understood all that.'

'It means that if you go away for any length of time, I don't know how we can do this. And it was me who told you not to stay locked up inside and to go out and live a bit . . .' He looks at his watch hurriedly and I can tell that he really does have to be somewhere else this evening, but the problem he's just broached means he won't be able to leave as quickly as he would have liked.

'I don't think I'll be going anywhere exotic in the immediate future, if that helps at all,' I say, trying to quell his fears.

As he returns all his equipment to his bag, he looks relieved and places a hand on my shoulder. 'At the same time, I want you to be out there enjoying yourself. Please just give me a call if you feel like going away again. Depending on where you choose to go, perhaps I'll know a doctor there who I can trust to do this.'

He is already at the front door and looking at his watch again. I manage to catch him up just as he steps out on to the landing.

'Doctor?'

'Yes?' I can sense that he's torn between cutting me off so he can make a quick getaway and the compassion he has always shown since giving me my final diagnosis.

'I just wanted to ask you . . . about my state of health . . . Is everything going as you thought . . . or . . .?'

I've managed to surprise him again and he looks at me curiously. 'I'm worried about misunderstanding you here,' he says. 'Do you want to know if the time frame I've given you has been extended? Is that what you're asking me?'

'That's what I'm asking.'

'OK. Well, as things stand, I'd say you're not doing too badly at all. You could, despite the treatment, be showing signs of fatigue or suffering. But that doesn't seem to be the case. So yes, you may have gained a little more time. I think we should look into doing some further tests and examinations. I promise you, we'll take the opportunity to talk about it at length next time.' He steps into the lift but stops the doors from closing. I just knew he would. 'I really do believe that your break in Brittany did you the world of good.'

'Thanks,' I reply, before turning back into the flat.

When I return to Chloé, she looks me up and down and seems almost panicky.

'Has he gone?'

'Yes! Stop worrying!'

Obviously in some sort of attempt to calm her nerves, she's taken up my favourite position on the sofa and has switched on the TV. *Money Drop* is on – one of my favourites.

'Did it feel like I was gone ages?'

'No, not really. I spent the time trying to find out what it is about this show you like so much. But I don't get it.'

I look at her in disbelief as I switch off the TV. 'It's too complicated to explain. Don't bother yourself. That's why I didn't insist we watch it at the spa.'

'And that was the right decision! I think I'd have just ditched your arse there and come back to Paris. How are you feeling, anyway?'

'Fine, for the moment. I should be just dandy for the next couple of hours. Shall we carry on?'

'To be honest, I'd rather you just relaxed, and we can look at all this when you're more up to it.'

'If you want. No problem. But there's something else I wanted to talk to you about. You can give me five minutes, can't you?'

'Erm . . . yes. Of course I can.'

She hesitates for a fraction of a second before she agrees. I sense that she knows I'm about to tackle a subject she has no desire to talk about, but I try to gather my thoughts. However, the last thing Lazreg said is playing on my mind. This deadline of mine – excuse the pun – that I more or less accepted a month ago now seems so very unfair. And I don't think my holiday did me the world of good, despite what he said.

But I try to put these thoughts to one side as I work out how to word my question to Chloé. 'I was going to ask you if it would be possible to meet some of the other members of your "organisation", or however you put it.'

I barely finish my sentence before she rears up, looking like she's ready to tell me where to go . . . or, worse, run out without a word.

But she responds. 'That was never even on the cards, and I can't think of a single reason why we'd change our minds on the subject now.'

There's something violent in her voice. I don't recognise her. Being the coward that I am, I search in vain for something to say to appease her, to get her to forget what I've just asked and to bring the conversation back to what it was. But she doesn't give me the time for any of that.

'Can I ask what your motives are? Do you want to change intermediaries? I can ask for someone else to be sent . . .'

'No! That's nothing to do with it . . .'

'Why, then? What's this about?'

She's too good at this for me and I know that, even if I could spin a line on occasion, I'd still not be able to get the better of her.

She starts again. 'I'm listening, Régis.'

I can see that she's on the verge of heading out and never coming back. I really need to explain myself.

I try . . . clumsily. As clumsily as one can, in fact. 'It's just that . . . because . . . this woman . . . that we're meant to . . .'

'Yes? What about her?'

'Well . . . with Reimbach, it was easier for me to . . . fall into line. But with this woman . . . I don't know her, and you haven't actually told me all that much. And I was thinking that maybe someone . . . one of the people you work with . . . hates her for some other reason, or knows something else about her, and that I'd be better off hearing it from them directly.'

There is so little conviction in my words that I prepare myself for a severe telling-off. But I get away with it. I watch as she pinches her lower lip between her thumb and index finger. She is weighing up the pros and cons, thinking how to respond without losing too much face.

'I can understand that,' she says after a long moment's hesitation. 'But I was supposed to be the only one of us you ever met.'

'Ah . . .'

'Listen, here's what I suggest. Let's start work on this, but I'd like you to make up your own mind as we go along. If after watching her for a while you still doubt our judgement on this, then I will try to get someone else to meet you. Does that sound OK?'

'Yes. Why not . . .'

I'm relieved. I want to continue this discussion. I want her to tell me more about this woman, but I still feel somewhat distracted by Lazreg and his visit.

Always tuned in to how I might be feeling or what mood I'm in, Chloé is already heading towards the front door to give me some peace. I have an urge to grab hold of her, to convince her to stay a little longer – just a little longer. But I don't want her to see me weakened or diminished. These are all new feelings for me – this desiring the company of another . . . This need to be careful of the impression I make.

She must have cast some sort of spell on me. Surely these emotions just aren't possible. I let her go without another word.

Chapter 12

The tops of the tower blocks at La Défense disappear into the brooding clouds above. The atmosphere in the capital has been unbearably sultry since this morning, with every single Parisian hoping that the storm on the horizon will give us some breathable air at last.

I'm on my fourth day of tracking her. Four days of watching every step taken by Stéphanie Tisserand and I am bored to death. I camp outside her flat from the early hours of the morning. I wait inside my little rented Renault Twingo until she leaves her garage at 8.30 a.m. – which she does, every morning, without fail. I follow her to her offices in Neuilly, on Avenue Charles-de-Gaulle, and then I wait. I sometimes take a quick stroll along the covered promenade or I sit in a nearby cafe until lunchtime. The first day, she drove to Les Quatre Temps shopping centre, where she grabbed a sandwich between trips to two *prêt-à-porter* stores. The day before yesterday, she just left the building and skipped across the road to get a pre-prepared salad from Monoprix and took it back to her office to eat. And yesterday, she met up with a female friend and the two of them went swimming at the nearby pool. The afternoons tend to be a little more exciting. I often have trouble keeping up with her in the Paris traffic. Sometimes she takes the ring road from Porte de Versailles, other times from the Palais des Congrès. Or she drives straight through Paris to some chic address or other in one of the better neighbourhoods. I imagine she's attending professional meetings, but I don't really know. She then heads back to her office and resurfaces again at around 7 p.m. in sports gear to set out on a run down the banks of the Seine as far as the Île de Puteaux. I must have made the resolution to start jogging at least a hundred times to rid myself of my extra pounds, so I have to admire the consistency of her efforts.

Then she goes straight home. On the first night, she didn't leave until the following morning. On the next night, I had to hide out in front of a swanky restaurant on one of those barges moored outside the Trocadéro until 11 p.m. She dined there with a couple who I can only describe as looking entirely unremarkable. Last night, she met up with an elegant-looking man, who also looked as innocent as they come, in front of the Théâtre Tristan-Bernard, where they saw a stand-up comedian. I had to buy a ticket. I forget the name of the guy, of course. All I remember is that I didn't laugh once.

The whole time, I'm on the lookout for her protection – trying to spot a meaty-looking man in her vicinity. As I follow her, I'm always checking the rear-view mirror for other vehicles that might be in her entourage. Around her building and outside her offices, I do the same. Where's the sinister face of the Georgian mercenary or Moldovan hitman I'm hoping to find? There's nothing. And she never looks worried. She doesn't even come across as being particularly vigilant. I never see her looking over her shoulder as she steps into her car or heads out to a public place. I'm actually finding the whole exercise rather tedious and I start asking myself what I'm even doing. This is a far cry from the adventure Chloé first promised me.

Perhaps it doesn't help my mood that I haven't seen her for a few days. I called her to let her in on the doubts I'm having about this seemingly never-ending pursuit that's leading nowhere, but our exchange was brief. She simply asked me to remain patient and to trust her. I told her that at no time had Stéphanie Tisserand behaved in any way that would suggest she was into any kind of activity of an unsavoury nature. She scoffed sarcastically. Before hanging up, she simply said, 'If that's what's bothering you, just wait a little longer and you'll soon see what you're up against.' That was yesterday, and nothing's happened since.

The barman in Le Passage recognises me now. He sees me getting out of my car at almost the exact same time every morning. I sit at the same table with a book, a newspaper and a couple of scientific reviews. He gives me a white coffee and I pretend to be engrossed in my reading while actually never taking my eyes off number 151 – her office building. Occasionally, he asks me to free up the table, so I place another order. I alternate between coffee and orange juice. I settle the bill as soon as the drink is placed in front of me, just in case I have to make a swift exit. Every two hours, I have to leave and top up the parking meter just a few yards up the avenue. It's never too far away and I've been lucky enough so far not to lose my table. Whenever I leave for good, I can sense the suspicious look the waiter gives me. It's something I can almost physically feel on the back of my neck. If it's ever on the news that something dreadful has happened to the nice woman who works across the road, he'll call the police and inform them about my odd behaviour. That's a given. My lack of conviction in this mission means I'm forgetting about being careful. I'm not taking the most basic of measures. This isn't very professional, seeing as I'm supposed to be a contract killer. Well, a part-time contract-killer.

I don't see her leave this lunchtime. What I do see is a caterer delivering around a dozen meal trays. Perhaps she has a meeting with clients or some of her staff? So I stay where I am. This means I have to order a steak with Béarnaise sauce and chips. Obviously. Professor Lazreg told me that I might experience a loss in appetite, but that doesn't seem to be the case at all.

It's now 4 p.m. I've just finished reading a rather thorough article on the question of whether or not an antiquark might be present in the composition of a pentaquark. No doubt unconcerned by the absurdity of such a theory, the barman is having a quick snooze behind the counter. He'd been polishing the same glass for at least ten minutes.

Logically, I have another three hours to wait before my target leaves her office for her daily exercise. And so I wait, hoping for an exciting turn of events and not just the same old routine from Stéphanie.

My wish is granted when just a few seconds later I see her leaving the building. Her car is parked across the road, but she doesn't go anywhere near it. I'm not sure what to do next. I watch as she waits on the pavement and looks at the passing cars carefully. I realise that this means she's waiting to be picked up. I'm going to have to get to my Twingo fast if I want to know what happens next.

I leave the cafe, muttering a quick goodbye, and scurry out to get to my car.

It has to be over forty degrees in this tin can and the air conditioning only kicks in after a few minutes. I can't stop looking at Stéphanie Tisserand and my eyes are literally burning.

This is the first time I detect a little anxiousness in her face. She continues to watch the cars as they pass and every few seconds she looks down at her mobile. Perhaps she's checking the time, or reading messages?

From where I'm parked, I can take a good look behind me at every car before it reaches her. Not a single one slows down. Nobody seems to be looking for anything . . . or anyone. Except, maybe . . .

There's a five-door Porsche approaching now. I can't make out the driver himself but I clock the way he's behaving. It's what I was hoping to see. He slows down, but he's not looking for somewhere to park. I'm sure of it. As he draws level with me, I notice that his number plates are Dutch. No, from Luxembourg. I thought I might be able to see who was behind the wheel, but I'm still a little wet behind the ears and the windows are, of course, tinted. There's not a chance of seeing anything that's going on inside that car.

My intuition is right. Stéphanie Tisserand looks like she recognises the vehicle, and when it stops in front of me, I watch her cross the road, walk around it and lean into the passenger window, which is now rolled down. There isn't even the hint of a smile on her lips as she gets in beside the driver. They drive off. I follow them, fingers crossed. I hope against hope that they don't take the motorway. I don't know if I'm up to this.

I watch as they make a U-turn on the roundabout on the Pont de Neuilly and head back in the direction of Paris. I feel semi-reassured at this point. When I notice that they're not going anywhere near the ring road and are instead about to take Avenue de la Grande Armée, I know that we're not about to travel the length of France this afternoon and feel relieved. As we approach Place Charles de Gaulle, I reduce the distance separating my car from the Porsche. Innumerable roads lead off this roundabout, so I can't afford to leave any room for surprises, though I very much doubt they'll spot me in such a sea of traffic. We cross the immense intersection and continue down the Champs-Élysées before branching off on to Avenue Montaigne a little further down. They blend perfectly into the background in the Porsche. The designer boutiques flash by and I feel like we're not too far from our destination . . .

I'm not wrong. The indicator flashes orange and the Porsche slips into a side street and parks up on the Plaza Athénée. A valet rushes out of a huge hotel to greet them, but a man – who I had no inkling was there – beats him to it and gets out of the back of the car to open the door for Stéphanie Tisserand. As she steps out, I note that she's not really giving off a friendly vibe; at least, she's smiling a lot less than she was in the photos.

The driver joins them. He is tall and slim, but the way he moves and holds himself betrays his age. He's knocking on a bit. Anyone can see that. He's wearing sunglasses and a black fedora in plaited straw – the summer version. His collar-length grey hair confirms his years. He hands the key over to the valet and joins Stéphanie as they walk up the wide flight of stairs to the doors of the hotel. I don't manage to see his face. The two of them walk into the building, but the first man – who, I've just noticed, is disconcertingly imposing in stature – stays on the pavement, standing away from the hotel staff with his hands behind his back and looking from side to side. If he's not a bodyguard then he's doing a very good impression of one.

I'm looking desperately for somewhere to park but trying to go about it as calmly as I can. I'm feeling quite optimistic, though, even with the presence of this massive gorilla guy, because it looks like Stéphanie Tisserand's attitude has changed. This has got to mean something: the car . . . this place. She seems so much more serious than usual, more professional somehow. I can feel that there's something very challenging ahead of me now, and I'm excited. This has got to be an improvement on the last few days.

I have no idea how long they're going to be. What should I do with myself in the meantime? There's not a chance I can stay parked outside in a Twingo without drawing the attention of the hotel staff. I start circling, going up and down the surrounding streets in an effort to find somewhere to park. No luck. I'm going to have to stay stuck behind the wheel. I realise that now. I hover around a no-parking bay and reason that I can just move off if I'm in anybody's way.

I normally look down on drivers who keep their engines running when they're at a standstill, but I do it today. I need the air conditioning on. I don't think my environmentally unfriendly behaviour is too big a deal. The ozone layer isn't likely to be impacted greatly, because I see the black Porsche is on its way back already. The valet stops in front of the steps and Stéphanie and her friend exit the building. They're joined by two young women. I'm on the other side of the square at quite a distance, but even from where I am I can see that one is a blonde and the other a brunette – Asian, maybe. They're both extraordinarily beautiful. They climb into the back seat with Stéphanie Tisserand and the driver gets behind the wheel. The bodyguard comes out of nowhere and joins him in the front this time. I imagine it's quite a squeeze in there. And they're gone. I don't want to lose them so I'm going to have to get myself into gear. There are no police vehicles around that I can see, and the traffic isn't that heavy . . . So I go for it, and make a quick but risky

U-turn. I can see them at the end of the road. I'm only a couple of hundred metres behind them now. I look at the clock on the dashboard, feeling pretty pleased with myself. They can't have spent any more than twenty-five minutes in the hotel.

We start our zigzagging through the streets of Paris again. We're back on the Champs-Élysées, and then Place Charles de Gaulle. I imagine we're returning to Neuilly, but we don't take Avenue de la Grande Armée as we circle the Arc de Triomphe; instead we head down Avenue Foch.

Am I having a lightbulb moment here? I remember coming down this street one evening and being shocked that the city's most expensive location, at least on the Monopoly board, was *the* place to go for high-class prostitutes. Is this just a coincidence? Or are we here for that very reason?

I think I have my answer. The Porsche indicates and pulls in next to the pavement. My initial instinct is to do the exact same thing, but I know that parking is forbidden here, and I can't afford to draw any attention to myself. So I overtake and reduce my speed as much as I can. I have no other option but to continue down the street and try to watch what I can through my mirrors. The driver has put on the hazard warning lights. A door opens. The back door. One of the two younger women gets out. It's the blonde. I can see her a lot more clearly than before, and she's no woman. The term 'young girl' is definitely more appropriate. She's almost a child, in fact. She's slim – skin and bones, really – and the amount of make-up she's wearing is beyond belief. Her outfit is far too provocative for a girl of her age. She leans in towards the passenger window and makes a vague sign with her hand. Then the car is on the move once again.

She stands for a few seconds and watches as it leaves. I am overcome with a desire to stop my car, approach her and ask her what's going on. But I can't. What would I say? How could I even go about it?

'Hi there, Miss . . . I was just wondering . . . Are you a prostitute and have you just been selling your charms to horrible rich old men at the hotel on the Plaza Athénée?

I'm not sure how well that would go down. And anyway, until she says otherwise, the only thing I'm supposed to be doing for Chloé is following our target. This means I have to keep going. I continue down Avenue Foch at an average speed now. Not too fast, not too slow. The Porsche overtakes me before we reach Porte Dauphine and this time we take the ring road.

I slip into the traffic and worry that I won't be able to keep up with them, but the driver goes at a nice steady pace in the middle lane. I allow a couple of cars to get between us and we all continue to head north.

As we near Porte de la Chapelle, I get a slight scare. I watch them choose the right-hand lane. What's going on? Does this mean they're heading for the airport? They leave the ring road at the junction. What are we doing getting off here? The luxurious car will stick out like a sore thumb in this neck of the woods. We're halfway between Seine-Saint-Denis and the eighteenth arrondissement, and even putting aside all prejudices one might have about the residents of this neighbourhood, I don't think I'd feel particularly safe in a car like that around here. The driver puts on his hazard warning lights again and comes to a stop. So we're not going to the airport. That's something, at least. This time, my reactions are a little quicker and I park behind a small van so I can climb out and get a better look. There are quite a lot of cars parked nearby and some of them are not in the best condition. In fact, there are a couple that look like they've been parked here for years. And then I understand. I'm a bit slow on the uptake, you see. Some of these vans have been fitted out for a purpose – to receive punters. I dread to think what else I'm going to witness now.

And my fears are very quickly realised.

The Asian girl gets out of the Porsche. So it's her turn now. She doesn't look back once at Stéphanie Tisserand or her gentleman accomplice, but just crosses the road, quickening her pace as she nears the other side. She's teetering along in the highest of heels with a heavy-looking handbag swinging from her minuscule arm. Her silk skirt is unreasonably short, and I get a glimpse of the tops of her black stockings. As she reaches the other side of the street, she stops between two parked cars and lights up a cigarette.

Instinct tells me to abandon my pursuit of Stéphanie and I let the Porsche go on its way. I'm stuck now. Do I go and talk to the girl? My decision is made for me as a Volkswagen estate drives up to the girl and slows down. The driver, the very image of a decent family man, exchanges a few words with her. I can't imagine following them. I don't even want to know what this man's up to. So I start the engine and drive off back in the direction of the west of Paris.

It's only when I'm back in front of Stéphanie's Neuilly offices that I remember feeling a vibration in my pocket earlier. Before getting out of the car, I check the voicemail on my phone.

'*Her PA has just booked her a one-way ticket from Paris to Vilnius for Thursday evening and another seven tickets to Vilnius for Sunday. So we need to get this done before then. OK? Where are you?*

CHAPTER 13

I'm relieved to find they haven't yet arrived in Neuilly. I'm stretching my legs on the pavement when I see the Porsche coming back. Stéphanie Tisserand steps out of it almost before the car has come to a complete standstill. Immediately, I can see that she's a lot more relaxed and, for the first time, I feel like I'm dealing with someone with a kind of double personality. She's a pleasant, affable businesswoman in her nine-to-five life, and then in her down time she becomes this cynical, perverse creature involved in some of the worst activities out there. I watch her enter her office, her stride as jaunty as ever, and I head back to my table over at Le Passage. As I close the door behind me, a storm hits.

Rain pours down in sheets and doesn't let up for over twenty minutes. It hasn't rained for almost three weeks and the ground just can't soak up the water. It's a total deluge. Soon there are torrents gushing through the gutters, overflowing on to the pavement and roadway. The very few passers-by caught in the downpour rush to find shelter, their summer clothes immediately soaked and clinging to their skin, but I can still read on their faces a sense of relief at finally being released from the heavy, stifling atmosphere.

And of course, as soon as the storm has passed, the temperature becomes bearable again. We can all breathe, and I feel liberated.

I've decided not to get back to Chloé. Not immediately, anyway. It's gone 6 p.m. and unless this afternoon's events have somehow changed what she's up to today, I'm expecting the woman I've now seen in a very different light to come back out of her office any time now.

An idea strikes me. I remember her daily runs and the route she usually takes. She always goes up Avenue Charles-de-Gaulle, along the banks of the Seine and past the numerous houseboats that are moored there. She then crosses the bridge before completing two laps of the Île de Puteaux.

I also think about the type of clothing she usually wears. It's always so light – far too flimsy to conceal a weapon anywhere on her person. And I've really left no stone unturned. I've followed her for three days straight and I'm certain there's been no bodyguard anywhere near her. As Chloé said, she's only escorted when she's out and about in the underworld of prostitution or up to other shady dealings.

Last night, still hot on her heels, I also managed a full lap of the island. Without really thinking that it might come in handy at some point, I found two or three isolated spots, sheltered from any possible prying eyes, right by the dirty brown waters of the Seine. I took particular note of the southern tip of the island, just next to the floodgate at the foot of a bridge. There's a small area there, blocked from view by a building belonging to the French Waterways organisation and so close to the barrage of water coming from the floodgates that any possible noise would be covered up.

It's looking pretty solid. Now it just remains to be seen whether she'll take the same route she usually takes and, should the opportunity arise, whether I have the courage to act. Because I'm under no illusions here. Drowning someone is much more violent in nature than giving them an injection. Plus, and Chloé was right to mention this straight away, it's a woman this time. A woman who, until this afternoon, I wouldn't have suspected of the slightest wrongdoing.

I'll be in at the deep end soon enough. I don't have any time to waste and want to be sure of getting there ahead of her, so I leave the bar and return to my car. I do my best to avoid the puddles lingering on the tarmac and hope that this afternoon's storm hasn't dissuaded her from taking her evening jog.

From behind the wheel, I fiddle with my phone. I'm wavering on that resolution I made not to call Chloé. Should I tell her of my intentions and, if so, do I think she'd approve? I'm starting to doubt myself now. I know she's not a massive fan of improvisation. But the worst thing about all this? The only thing I'm actually giving any serious thought to is how to please her. It's as if I want to give her the death of Stéphanie Tisserand all wrapped up in pretty packaging, so we can move on to the next part of our little story. This is my sole aim. Should I be worried about that?

To help me with the waiting part, I switch on the car radio. Just as the news comes on, Stéphanie Tisserand walks out of her building. She is in her sports gear and heads off at a brisk pace towards La Défense. I start the engine.

It's impossible to find a parking space anywhere near the Puteaux bridge. It's now the third time I've driven up or down every nearby street without success. I know that it doesn't take her any more than quarter of an hour to get to this point; if I don't find somewhere soon, I'm done for. I've just driven down Boulevard Richard Wallace with no success (again) and I'm starting to lose patience when I spy a young woman on the pavement getting a bunch of keys out of her handbag. She presses a remote control on her keyring and the lights on a Twingo, not dissimilar to my own and parked just behind me, flash briefly as the car is unlocked. I slam the brakes on and start to reverse before questioning the woman with pleading eyes. She gives me the charitable smile that all motorists give their fellow drivers when they are freeing up a much-needed parking space. I watch her manoeuvre out, bumping the vehicle in front at least three times, before finally driving away.

Prudence forces me not to forget to pay for an hour's parking. If the police take an interest in little old me at some point in the future, it would be best not to have paper evidence in the form of a traffic warden's ticket proving that I was in this vicinity today.

As soon as I set foot on the island, an inexplicable reflex makes me turn around and look behind. There's no mistaking it. It's her. With her headphones on, she's wearing that little smile of hers that I've got so used to seeing. She's going a lot faster than when I saw her leaving her office. She's picked up her pace. This is good. This is what she always does once she's warmed up. It means she hasn't changed a single detail of her routine. Perfect. Logically, she should turn right when she gets off the bridge and she'll start her tour of the island in an anti-clockwise direction. If I turn left, I won't need to run faster than her to get to the spot I have in mind. In fact, I'll have plenty of time to get my act together. The first time she comes past will give me the chance to think it all through. The second time, I'll do it.

Less than five minutes later and I'm in position. The place is exactly as I remember it from last night. There are no houseboats or barges nearby. The bridge, which carries only pipelines and hydraulics, screens the right bank perfectly. And the building masks the left bank as well as the campsite in the Bois de Boulogne. The noise from the floodgates drowns out all sound within, I estimate, a hundred-metre radius of the site. Nobody could possibly guess what I'm working myself up to. And unless a barge or pleasure boat passes by, nobody can actually see me here.

I have a few minutes left to find the perfect lookout spot, so I can assure myself of Stéphanie Tisserand's exact movements. I notice a tree right next to the building. The trunk is definitely wide enough for me to comfortably hide behind. I check around for other joggers and make my way towards it.

And there I wait. I recognise her clothing in the distance and, as she nears me, I attempt to work out the distance between us. When she's almost parallel, I count out four of her steps and then note that, at this exact point, the angle is perfect. All I have to do is run up behind her and push her the four or five metres to the waiting river. She still has her earphones in and, if the volume of her music is as loud as I hope it is, combined with the racket of the water, she won't even hear me coming.

I don't take my eyes off her until she disappears down the footpath by the lock. I know that she runs at approximately eight kilometres an hour, which means that she'll be dead in less than half an hour. Because, strangely enough, I have not a single doubt remaining. Unless another jogger happens to come by at the exact same time as her, I'm doing this.

Just to pass the time, I try to work out how I acquired this certainty and how I managed to do away with my last remaining scruples. There's Chloé, of course. If that girl asked me to kill the Dalai Lama, I'd probably just get on with it, no questions asked. I don't know what that's all about. I'm not the kind of man who falls head over heels like this. Unless . . . It could just be that I've never really understood the emotional state of love. Maybe I am in love and I don't even recognise it for what it is. No, I need to be a little more dispassionate about all this. If I take Chloé out of the picture for the moment and focus solely on my prey, I easily reach the conclusion that I simply want to kill her. Not when I see her leaving her home in the mornings or looking around the shops. When I observe her in her typical daily life, I can't even conceive of laying a finger on her. If I stretch things a little, I might even describe her as pleasant. But there's also the side to her I witnessed today. I've never felt particularly comfortable during the physical act of love, so I cannot even begin to imagine the hell it must be to have to tolerate the advances of a perfect stranger, like you're just a cheap commodity. How does she manage to dominate her girls like that? Does she promise them a marvellous future when she goes around the world picking them up? Does she take their passports off them, like I've seen reported on TV documentaries? It doesn't matter how she does it. If everything goes as planned, in ten minutes' time, I'm convinced I'll be sparing myriad young girls from a despicable end.

I can see the movement of a runner now. But they're too fast. Too light on their feet. And it's too soon. It can't be her. I take another quick look, just to be sure. I don't recognise the clothing. It's a man. He's finely built, toned, and doesn't seem to have a scrap of fat under his copper-coloured skin. It's as if he's running on air. I bet he has an excellent marathon record. At the speed he's going, it'll be a good idea to just get out of here, because it won't take him long to get back if he laps the island again. He'll be the one to find the body, I imagine. Unless there's a strong current . . .

I can see someone else coming. I don't need to check this time. I know it's her. She runs past me. And just like before, I count out four steps. And then I launch myself at her.

She turns at the last moment as I throw my arm around her head and shove my left hand over her mouth to stop her from screaming. She looks terrified, but I ignore that. I'm already forcing her towards the riverbank and she's losing her balance. I'm using all my weight to push her forward and still keep her on her feet. We reach the edge.

One final push and I tip her over into the river. I lie on my stomach on the wet quayside, still holding on to her body and pushing her head under the water with my hand. She struggles but can't escape my grip. I add a little more pressure, and with my free hand I try to stop her arms from flailing. I look around me briefly. Not a soul. I hear a muffled cry come from the water as a few bubbles rise to the surface. She's defending herself, but the energy she's putting into it is lessening. A minute or so later and only the odd jolt comes from her limp frame. I keep her head under the surface for a few seconds longer and then congratulate myself on the speed of the operation.

It's done. She's now just an inert mass, which I'm about to hand over to the flow of the river. I slide away from the bank after giving her one last push, and then I stand up. Her sports clothing is in shades of khaki-green; a beautiful camouflage in the murky waters of the Seine, I think. There's no way she's immediately recognisable as human, that's for sure. I look down at my own outfit, tuck my shirt into my trousers and try to rub away the odd muddy stain. I walk down the deserted towpath alongside several abandoned barges and look up towards the bridge. There's not a soul in sight. I glance between two of the boats and can see the outline of Stéphanie Tisserand's body. It's floating away from me in the direction of Levallois-Perret. I'll be able to call Chloé now.

Chapter 14

'I'm not sure you've done the right thing.'

When I call her straight after the deed, I'm hoping for a small gasp of surprise, a hint of approval in her voice or even a compliment on my initiative. But there's none of that. On the contrary; she declares that we have to see one another as soon as is humanly possible. And by the time I get back home from Neuilly, she's already waiting for me.

When we're settled down in my living room, things are unmistakably frosty. On her part, in any case. She begins by asking me why I took it upon myself to act the way I did without first consulting her, and I quickly understand that my basic 'because I felt like it' argument isn't going to wash with her and will only feed the anger she's trying so desperately to contain. I'd rather just get it over with, so I confirm with unexpected insolence that I just couldn't let an opportunity like that pass me by; that if I hadn't done it, we'd maybe have had to wait a long time, and that the idea of saving more innocent victims gave me the boost I needed to act quickly. And that it was an unmitigated success. Again.

Upon her request, I go into every last detail as to how I went about it and the precautions I took. She is clearly suspicious. She wants to know if I thoroughly checked that there was no video-camera surveillance, and if there really were no eyewitnesses who might be able to place me on that island at the time of death. Despite my every effort, and several arguments in which I think I come across as very convincing, the only thing she says to me is, once more, 'I'm not sure you've done the right thing.'

And if only it could stop there, it might not be so bad. But no. There's more where that came from.

'Do you remember what happened to that man? After the job you turned down?'

'The elite soldier?'

'Yes, the elite soldier. Do you want to end up like him? Shot to pieces like a rabbit?'

All I can do is look at her sheepishly as I reply. 'Of course not.'

'Please,' she continues in what strikes me as an excessively stern voice, 'don't take such a childish tone with me.'

I cringe at this.

Although it's true that I haven't always known how to behave around people, I still realise that here I have no choice but to feign indifference and wait for the thunderstorm to pass. So I keep my mouth shut and walk to the kitchen to fetch two beers without asking her if she wants one. I place hers in her hand and state simply that, seeing as we have nothing to celebrate, there won't be any Moët & Chandon this evening, just a simple 1664. I score a point with this, and the briefest of smiles crosses her lips.

Then, just a couple of moments later, she cracks.

'It's fine,' she says, holding out her bottle. 'I'm sorry for getting cross with you.'

I pretend to hesitate before clinking my 1664 against hers to seal our reconciliation.

She adds, 'I'm just frightened that you'll get caught and we won't be able to carry on with this. You have to admit that it would be a shame, wouldn't it? I want us to keep at it!'

I have trouble sharing her enthusiasm. I'm feeling a little sceptical about the whole business now, and she notices this. She asks what the problem is.

'You know,' I say after a moment's thought, 'I can't say that this has been the most exciting week of my life. I've spent hours and hours sitting in a cafe, and I've driven a few kilometres around Paris in a Twingo. Even I've had better adventures than that in my time. So maybe I just wanted to speed things up a bit. It was starting to feel too drawn out.'

My assessment appears to amuse her. After asking a few more questions about how exactly I've been spending my time over the last few days, she admits that getting rid of Arthur Reimbach was no doubt a lot more 'entertaining' but that there was a moral contract in place and it wasn't really up to me to choose my victims, but rather her and her associates. I admit that this is true, and add only that it would suit me greatly if perhaps we could spend a little less time preparing in future and move on from one case to the next with greater speed.

'Christ alive! I hardly recognise you! Do you remember what you said to me back when I first came to talk to you? You said you were just a scientist who wanted to live as a recluse in his flat and that there were bound to be others out there more suited to murdering than you. And now you're wanting to step it up?'

'Yes, well . . . There's no need to exaggerate. I just mean that if I'm going to play your game and risk spending what time I have left behind bars, then the game had better be worth playing.'

She looks at me now with an unbearable air of triumph, which, as I've noticed before, she exudes every time she feels a victory is hers. She gives me one of her delicious smiles again and I just can't stand it.

'Let's turn the page on Stéphanie Tisserand, OK?' she says. 'I just want you to guarantee me that you didn't take any risks, and we can be done with it.'

'I swear.'

'So, you want to move on swiftly to the next case, then?'

'Erm, yes. If that's at all possible.'

'I'll be back in a few days, OK? I'll let you know as soon as I've got something.'

'Are you going away?'

'Yes, but not far and not for long. Promise.'

◆ ◆ ◆

It's been five days and I've had no news from Chloé. And let's make no bones about it: it's been five days of misery either sat in front of my TV . . . or sat in front of my TV. This is a situation that would have suited me down to the ground only a few weeks ago, but now it weighs heavier on my soul than the two murders I've committed in the meantime.

The programmes on offer are just dire. It's the start of the school holidays and all my favourite games have been rescheduled to make way for sitcom repeats whose infantile humour would probably escape your average viewer, let alone someone like me.

I decide to follow the Tour de France instead. Every single second of it. It's a struggle, though.

Hours later and I'm now more than capable of reciting the list of teams and the names of all the leaders' managers. I'm also pretty much the expert on the right way to cook *ruifard de Valbonnais* or how to ripen Chabrirou du Velay cheese, for these are the sorts of interesting things you pick up in the commentating. I also manage to calculate to the nearest three seconds who will arrive in the top ten in the overall rankings, and the number of kilowatts released by each and every cyclist since leaving the Domancy coast.

So it's not like I'm allowing brain rot to set in, and I do manage to catch a little bit of daylight. In the mornings I venture outside to buy a baguette and other bits and pieces to eat, and one evening, uncharacteristically, I wander down Rue de Rennes to the Virgin store at Montparnasse. It's not that I have an irrepressible desire to buy a CD or read a book, it's just that I left my laptop there weeks earlier to be repaired and I think it's about time I picked it up. It's on this little expedition of mine that something worrying occurs . . .

I spot a family exiting the Saint-Placide Métro station. The man is up front with his hands in his pockets and seems indifferent to the woman, who I presume is his wife, walking a dozen or so steps behind him. In her left arm, she's carrying a little girl close to her body. The child can be no more than two or three years old and wears a distant, almost haunted look on her little face. In her other hand, the woman is holding a discount-supermarket carrier bag and it looks heavy – too heavy for her to manage properly.

The man turns back to look for his wife. She has stopped to put the child and the bag down on the ground so she can swap arms. I'm too far away to hear him, but I don't have to. I can tell from his gestures that he's hurling insults at her. I stop to watch the scene unfold and I notice that a young couple have stopped, too. The three of us watch as this man walks back to his wife and screams in her face just that little bit louder. He doesn't hit her. I suppose he knows better than to do that in public, but I can see by the way she flinches, lowers her head and moves her arms to protect her child that violence is something she knows intimately.

The couple and I look at one another. We are clearly all weighing up the idea of going over and saying something. But what? I think that, if things had gone a little further, the young man would have intervened. He looks the self-assured type and is certainly the right build. I would have helped him, no doubt – but I don't really know what I might have done. The nasty individual has already given up yelling at his wife by this point and is yards ahead of her again, leaving her with the toddler and the bag.

The young man and I exchange a second sorrowful glance and then his girlfriend pulls at his arm and they walk off in the direction of Saint-Germain-des-Prés. I too continue my journey towards Virgin, but after making my way across the road I have second thoughts. I turn back and search through the crowds, looking for that dreadful excuse for a man and his unfortunate little family.

I spot them in next to no time. They are walking down Rue de Vaugirard towards Boulevard du Montparnasse and I run to catch them up, narrowly avoiding being hit by the number 96 bus.

My pursuit of them doesn't last long. They turn down Rue de l'Abbé-Grégoire and disappear behind the door of a building that's half-obscured by scaffolding.

I don't go to Virgin. I stay put in front of that building until 9 p.m. I think I'm expecting some sort of drama, or for the man to come out on his own; in which case, I would have followed him again to find out a bit more about him. Who knows? Perhaps it's better that we don't understand my thought processes on this one.

Chapter 15

Chloé finally decides to let me know she's still in the land of the living. It's late evening when she calls. She starts by telling me how sorry she is for not having been in touch. Well, that bit's not true, really – what she actually does is laugh and take the mickey out of me, asking how much I've missed her. I do my best to ignore her jibes, which makes her laugh even more, and so, beaten, I admit to having wondered whether or not I'd ever see her face again.

'I promised you! And I always keep my promises,' she tells me. And then she adds, 'Unless I've got all my dates mixed up, it was yesterday that you had your treatment, wasn't it?'

'That's right.'

'And how was it? I imagine it was a long night?'

'It was just like it always is. I'm feeling better already.'

'So you'll be back on your feet in no time?'

'No doubt about it.'

'Come and meet me in Lille. There's a train that leaves every hour on the hour from the Gare du Nord. You tell me which one you're on and I'll come and pick you up. Come tomorrow.'

'Right . . . yes . . . But what are we going to . . .'

'It'll be a surprise!'

◆ ◆ ◆

She's waving at me like a mad thing as I step down to the platform at Lille Flandres station. As though I might miss her. She's like a shining beacon standing bang in the middle of the hundreds of passengers scurrying around her. A lot of them look annoyed, as most of the trains are running two hours late, including mine.

When I near her, I think for just a split second that she's going to put her arms around me, but she holds back and takes my arm, leading me outside.

'I didn't think you'd ever get here! Do you know what happened?'

'Something to do with some cables falling on the lines, it seems. But I had a thesis to read that one of my students handed in. The time just went.'

'I just don't know how people can spend so much of their lives buried in complicated things like theses. Oh, it doesn't matter. You're here now . . . Do you know Lille at all?'

'I've been once, but it was a long time ago. It was to take my wife to one of her cousins' weddings. All I remember is that everyone drank a lot, laughed very loudly, and that I had no clue what most of them were talking about.'

'You're unbelievable. Come on. Let's go. We're going to have a bite to eat first. I know a really nice little place and it never gets too crowded, so you'll survive.'

She isn't lying. It is a lovely place and I'm pleasantly surprised. We're in an old-fashioned brasserie with huge gold mirrors and elegant waiting staff. It's formal, but not too in-your-face. Chloé asks for a table in the back room, where only three others are occupied. We are at least four metres away from our nearest neighbours, which is a plus – as I'm sure we're about to embark on a highly confidential conversation. But we're not there yet. As we sit down, she addresses the waiter, who is holding out the chair for her.

'No need to bring us the menus,' she tells him. 'I'll have the Maroilles salad and my husband will have the full Welsh. And we'll have two beers. Pints.'

That's a lot of information for me to take in. I have to make a superhuman effort not to lose the plot as I ask her, tut-tutting, what exactly it is I'm about to eat.

'You're going to adore it! The Welsh is every disastrous food habit known to man, especially you, all in one go!'

'And what are these "disastrous" habits of mine?'

'Are you joking? You eat worse than a teen who lives above a McDonald's. It's all fried meat and crisps at your place! I just loved watching your face when anyone ever tried to give you vegetables when we were in Brittany!'

'All right, all right! So what am I about to eat, then?'

'It's like a toasted sandwich, drowning in melted cheddar, with a sausage and an egg on top. Served with chips, obviously.'

'If it wasn't already in the offing, I'd presume you want me dead.'

I already regret my attempt at a joke, but it just came to me and I know that Chloé doesn't mind me talking about death. But I ask her to forgive my clumsiness.

'Don't worry about it.'

Her face darkens, but she forces herself to give me an indulgent and compassionate look as she says, 'I don't blame you. I suppose it must be playing on your mind all the time, and every now and again it just has to come out.'

'I don't know. Let's talk about something else.'

'Well, haven't you got anything to ask me?'

'I don't think so.' I'm such a dreadful comedian. I try to show a healthy devil-may-care attitude, but I'm terrible at it. At least I manage to get a hint of a smile out of her.

'Come on! Ask me!'

I take the bait. 'When did we get married, then? Haven't we rather rushed into it?'

This time the expression on my face, which I adopt deliberately, makes her laugh out loud.

'It all depends on how you look at it.'

She's interrupted as the waiter returns to the table with a fully laden tray. There's far too much food for two people. He puts down our beers first, then the salad for madame before banging down the biggest plate of chips and a huge bubbling dish of God-knows-what swimming in oil. I've never paid much attention to my diet and I have even less reason to do so now, but the thought of ingesting all that seems unreasonable. I think I detect a touch of irony in his voice as he wishes us the standard '*Bon appétit!*'

He moves away and Chloé, who I can sense is almost shaking with impatience, jumps back to the case in point. 'Right! Let me tell you everything! And don't worry, I'll get straight to the point. This won't take long. In fact, you'll be home safe and sound by tonight, I imagine.'

'So . . . we're actually going to *do something* today . . .'

'Yes. This afternoon. I can even give you a precise time. We'll be *doing something* at 4 p.m. It's just that you'll need a bit of time to imagine yourself in the role of . . . well, it's something you've never done before.'

Hmm! I don't like the sound of this. She's approaching the whole thing with kid gloves, which means she knows I'm not going to be happy about whatever it is.

'Just explain what's what.'

'No need to panic. It's just that you're going to have to become a daddy.'

'What?'

'Relax, Régis. You're the father of an only child. OK? A boy. His name is Mathéo. He's nine years old and he's really sweet, but the poor kid's disabled, right? It's a shame, isn't it?'

'I hope I'm totally misunderstanding every word you're saying.'

Chloé laughs loudly. I can't see myself in any of the mirrors because they're too high when I'm sitting down, but I imagine my face is a real picture.

'Where is this kid, then?'

The laugh is even louder this time. 'Don't worry! You won't even see him.'

I still haven't the foggiest. I'm starting to find the whole conversion frustrating now. I decide to have a little sulk for a while and get stuck into my Welsh.

It's only when I've finished this heart attack on a plate (which obviously I love) that we start speaking again. Chloé supposes I'm not going to bother with a dessert, and she supposes right.

When she looks directly at me again, she appears in the best of moods. 'Come on, then, I'm listening. Tell me what you want to know.'

'Just explain it all a bit better about the kid.'

'It's no biggie. Just calm down. We just need to pass for parents wanting to send their child to the local school. That's all there is to it. What else?'

'But who is it?'

'The name of the person we're going for? You'll never have heard of him.'

'But perhaps I'd like to know why he's in the firing line?'

'All in good time . . .'

Our coffees arrive. To make sure the waiter doesn't eavesdrop, we embark on a brief conversation about Belgian beer. He recommends a beer brewed at the Abbaye de Oudkerken, and as soon as he's gone we get back to business.

'He's called Guy Brison. He was thirty-two years old back in 1991, when he was arrested following a crime of a sexual nature. At the time, he was a primary school teacher here in Lille and the crime took place at his place of employment . . . I don't think I need to elaborate, do I?'

'That won't be necessary.'

'But nothing ever came of it and we don't know why. We suspect that pressure was put on the magistrate from someone up high. Probably someone with the same predilections. But we were never able to prove anything. All that happened is that he was moved to a different school – somewhere in the south of the country.'

'And where is he now?'

She seems satisfied with my level of interest and answers in a suitably disgusted tone. 'He came back to the region in 2003. He's still a teacher. Actually, he's a head teacher now at a primary school in Villeneuve-d'Ascq. It's not far from here.'

'And do you think it's still going on?'

She hesitates slightly before giving me a response. She is a lot less categorical than she's been in the past. 'He's never been pulled up for it, but there are definite doubts. Plus, he always spends his holidays in Thailand, and I don't think that's a coincidence.'

'OK! So you've decided to do . . . what's required.'

'This isn't a personal thing. Other people in my group have talked to me about him and I took some time to study his case, and I agree with them. It's gone on for too long and the powers behind me have helped set this up.'

'I see.' It's a pretty matter-of-fact response, given that I've just been informed that within mere hours I'll be killing again. I do need a few more details, though, willing as I am. 'What about the set-up?' I continue.

'It's very straightforward. School finished at the end of last week, but he's still working until the end of this week. There's a heap of admin to do and the budget to sort out and all the rest of it. We are parents. Mathéo's parents. He is disabled. We want him to start at the school in September. He's going to need a support worker and a whole range of equipment. We're having a meeting with him this afternoon to talk over our needs.'

'That all sounds fine. And what do we do when we get there?'

'He'll be on his own. The other teachers, the secretary and the two dinner ladies are all on holiday. We'll inject him. I managed to get hold of a product that I'm told works very well. It kills really quickly. It'll look like a heart attack – the great thing is, the chemical doesn't show up in a post mortem. And it can be injected into muscle. So it's going to be a lot easier than last time. I'll just distract him, and you do the rest. He'll more than likely put up a fight for a few seconds, but then that'll be it.'

I watch her closely. She is so convinced and so full of good intentions, even when it comes to wiping someone off the face of the earth. How could I fail to follow her? She knows it, too. She leans down to the floor to get something out of her handbag. She discreetly shows me a little black case. I recognise it. It's the same one we used for Arthur Reimbach.

'I've already prepared the needles and syringes. You need to keep all this with you until you get back to Paris. I think it's wise to do it that way. There's more chance of me being stopped by the police in my car than you on a train.'

'We're not going back together?'

'Nope. As soon as we've finished, I'll drop you off at the station. I'll go back on my own – via Belgium. I don't want us to be seen together. Just in case.'

'Fine. If you think that's best,' I say, disappointed.

'I'll be back with you in Paris in no time. Promise.' She looks down at her mobile on the table to check the time. 'Let's pay up and get out of here.'

'Right you are.'

Chapter 16

It takes us at least half an hour to pick up her car and drive out to Villeneuve-d'Ascq in the suburbs of Lille. The school we're heading to is a huge, austere-looking building at the end of a quiet little street dotted with pretty red-brick houses.

When Chloé pulls up and switches off the engine, we can't hear a sound. There isn't a soul around. The school playground has been empty for almost a week. The kids are all at home now, deafening their parents and making their lives a misery, no doubt. We make our way slowly over to the gates. He's left them half-open, perhaps for us; we haven't taken two steps into the playground when we hear his voice calling out.

'Monsieur and Madame Schneider?'

We look up to see where it's coming from and see his head sticking out of a first-floor window just above the main entrance. His face looks severe, his eyes mean, and his salt-and-pepper hair is cut too short.

'Come on in and it's the staircase on your left.'

There's very little warmth to his voice. I'm sure it must be something to do with being impatient to get his work over and done with, so he can go out to Pattaya and see his other children.

I feel my heart skip a beat as I push open the door. I don't think these places have blackboards and chalk any more, but the smell is just as I remember. I can still recall the endless hours of torture I experienced in a building not dissimilar to this, all those years ago; torture inflicted upon me by my so-called 'classmates'. Mates they were not. They made my life hell. They did the same to the teachers. But they singled me out because of my IQ and used any excuse to humiliate me.

The headmaster is waiting for us at the top of the stairs. He's shorter than I thought he would be. He is stocky with little legs – quite ugly, in all honesty. He's wearing a grey velour jacket that only the oldest and most weirdy-beardy types would have dared try to get away with even back in my day. I don't have a good feeling about this.

'Monsieur Brison, the headmaster of this school,' he bellows at us, holding out his hand.

I wouldn't be at all shocked if he clicked his heels together, military style. I'm a bit disappointed when he doesn't.

'My office, please,' he adds, inviting us to follow him.

The room is like the man. Old and grey. There's a map of the world above his chair on the back wall and I'm surprised that the USSR and French Equatorial Africa aren't on it.

'So . . . you are the parents of . . . erm . . .' He leans forward and picks up a folder. 'Mathéo, is that right?'

'That's right,' replies Chloé with a cheerful grin.

He takes a seat without asking us to follow suit, but we sit down anyway.

'Right, then. What's wrong with him, then – your son?'

Even though I know we're talking about an imaginary boy, the brutality of his question leaves me flabbergasted. I've never wanted kids. I'm not even curious about what it'd be like to have one, but who would dare speak to the parents of a disabled child like this? Chloé is just as shocked. I can see it on her face. And I don't think the teacher fails to spot it either.

'I don't tend to sugar-coat things. Sorry about that. It's just that I'd rather be honest with you. Having a cripple here at the school could be a source of great worry, not only for me, but for the teaching staff. It's problematic. There're not only the safety aspects to consider, but the worry of how he would get on with his fellow pupils . . . You know . . . cohesion. And then we'd have to swap about all the extracurricular activities, too.'

I can see that Chloé is about to pounce. She couldn't be any angrier if the man were talking about her actual son. 'But the school board has given its approval and they've already spoken to me about a classroom assistant,' she says between gritted teeth.

'Yes, so that's one more member of staff for me to have to manage. It's all well and good for the school board to be making these decisions. For them, a handicapped boy is just a file and a number that needs to be rubber-stamped. I'm the head of this establishment and I'm going to have to deal with all the extra work it entails.'

'Well, actually, the law demands that you . . .'

'Don't worry yourself about it. I know that I'm obliged to accept your child come September, so please, let's just try to make this easier on everybody. What am I to expect with him?'

This man isn't just a bitter old fool, he's a dangerously nasty piece of work. I find myself thinking back to Chloé's words when she first came over to my flat. She said, 'You'll see that these are people nobody will miss', and she was so right about that. No normal human being could regret hearing about this dreadful person's passing. Nobody.

We'd said that Chloé would distract him while I did what needed to be done. I've been fingering the two syringes in my pocket for a couple of minutes now. I stand up. Brison must be hoping that I'm on my way out and about to take my troublesome wife with me. But I am instead trying to give him the impression that I'm reflecting on what has just been said. I pace a little, put my head into my hands and rub my eyes. I'm trying out the shattered-father look, worn out by all the obstacles and constant struggles in my life. I walk behind his desk slightly to take a closer look at the map. Guy Brison turns to watch me. It's as though he's worried I'm about to explode at any moment. Reassured, however, that I'm simply lost in thought, he returns his gaze to Chloé. And I make my fatal move. I pull out one of the needles and plant it in his neck. He has enough time to let out a scream before I clasp my other hand over his mouth. It's such a pathetic, high-pitched little noise that nobody could have heard it. I quickly feel the weight of his head against my arm. There's no reaction from him. I push his body forwards. His cheek hits the file on my 'wrong' son with a thud. I pull out the needle and check for a pulse. Nothing. He's dead. I have no doubt about it. I'm getting quite good at making that diagnosis now. No need for the second syringe.

Chloé hasn't moved. I can see a definite hint of satisfaction and, dare I say it, I think she's impressed.

We pause to listen but can't hear a thing, other than a few birds chirruping in the playground. She gets up and we leave the office and trot down the stairs. There's nobody outside. Chloé gets back behind the wheel and I check to make sure there are no nosy neighbours twitching any curtains.

It's 4.15 p.m. Back to Paris, then.

On the way to the station, I check my phone for the train times. I'm going to have a job on. There's no way I'll make it in time to catch the next one and I'm going to have to wait almost an hour for the one after that. Just as we're arriving at Lille Flandres station, I explain this to Chloé and suggest that we go for a drink together, to help me pass the time; but she refuses. No reason. She's congratulated me on what I've just done, for how efficient I was – but no more than that. Not a word.

I find myself alone at the bar in a soulless station cafe with a *panaché*. Fortunately, one of the regulars asks the owner to put on the big flat-screen so he can watch the last stages of the Tour. This entertains me for a while, but not long enough. I decide to pay up and go for a walk, without venturing too far from the station. As I stand up, I feel a light pain, a strain really, under my left arm. I've been worrying about a lump that I found there yesterday evening. I'll talk to Lazreg about it next Tuesday. Maybe.

Once outside, I lift my head to the sky. It's dark grey with heavy, menacing clouds, which doesn't bode well for the rest of the day.

◆ ◆ ◆

In exchange for my reservation code, I get the ticket I've pre-booked on my phone out of a machine. Departure is in ten minutes and I can already see the train waiting at the platform. I board it and settle down into my first-class seat. I would never ordinarily allow myself this kind of luxury, but I need the peace and quiet today. I can't be dealing with any bothersome people at the moment.

CHAPTER 17

There aren't many people in my carriage, but there are enough to get on my nerves. Two men and two women in impeccably tailored clothing are particularly annoying. They're probably part of some sales team, off to an important conference or something equally dreadful. They're talking too loudly, especially the older man who I bet is the team leader, maybe even the commercial director or some other meaningless title. Whoever he is, the other three all force out extra-loud laughs whenever he makes a joke. They must be the only ones who get his wit, because everyone in the carriage can hear him and they're managing to contain themselves. We've only been on this train for ten minutes and I've already had enough.

The woman sitting next to me is just as exasperating. She's beautiful, but she knows it. She pretended to be not quite strong enough to put her bag up on the luggage rack. She obviously thought it completely natural that I would want to help her, and hardly thanked me when I did. Since we left the station, she has done her best to look elsewhere whenever I've lifted my eyes from the paper I'm marking. She's definitely one of the sorts I know I won't miss when I shed this mortal coil.

The sales team makes its way towards the bar, I assume, guffawing at nothing every step of the way. It's grotesque. One of the men must have doused himself in cologne this morning. It's coming off him in waves. He hits my elbow on his way past. He's one of the thoroughly irritating people I was hoping to avoid by paying more. He doesn't even apologise.

I wait a couple of minutes. I don't even bother gathering my belongings together. I just leave all my papers on top of my laptop, along with my phone, and follow them.

The bar is two carriages down from mine and, as I expected, there stands the little sales group. The boss guy is paying for two beers and two fruit juices, which the stewardess is placing down on the counter with a fake smile. One of the women struggles to carry the drinks over to a table. The other two are laughing at her as she tries to keep her balance. The big boss pockets his change and turns to join in the fun. 'Let's hope your sales figures go up, because I can't see you being much cop at a crappy waitress job!'

From behind her counter, the stewardess rolls her eyes slightly. She must see men like him and hear their tedious remarks day in, day out. I imagine it washes over a person eventually.

'What would you like, sir?' she asks, her selling smile back on her face.

'I'd like to kill that sorry excuse for a man' is what immediately comes to mind, but instead I order a beer.

'Cashews? Cookies? We've got a meal deal with . . .'

She goes through the motions of reciting everything. No doubt she works on commission. I think I'll leave her a tip. I decline her suggestions and she puts my can of beer down alongside a plastic glass.

I nod my head in the direction of the foursome to my left and whisper, 'Are all your customers that charming?'

'Ha! I don't take any notice these days. Especially not of him.'

'Do you know him?'

She leans in and whispers too. 'He makes a return trip every Thursday. He's always trying to chat us all up. He's a real old perv. When we receive our timetables for the week, it's always the first thing we look at – who's going to have to put up with this guy!'

'So it's hard going?'

She lowers her voice even further. 'I have a colleague who was thinking about going to the police about him. He put his hand up her skirt. Management convinced her not to do it, to avoid a scandal.'

Two other customers have just turned up and are waiting behind me. I thank the young woman and leave her the change from my €10 note. She looks very surprised and checks that I haven't made a mistake. Perhaps I shouldn't have done that; she'll remember me now. And if anything should happen on this train . . .

I move away from the counter and take a few steps towards the carriage wall and the windows. I pretend to be reflecting on the stark countryside whizzing past at 280 kilometres an hour and watch the old pervert in the reflection of the glass. I'm also listening to him. He's bragging to his colleagues about how he made the new trainee girl all hot and bothered as they left their meeting this afternoon. He really is a disgrace.

The conversation then moves on to how it's the company anniversary soon and how they'll all be going out to celebrate at Paradis Latin. This sad little man goes on and on about how he can get any woman he wants at this club, and how much he loves the place. I'm just about to leave him to it when – and there's no such thing as chance in this life – this lovely little snippet reaches my ears: 'She's safe, at least. I wouldn't touch a black girl with anyone's *barge pole*! I'd have to be gagging.'

I don't need to know who he's referring to. Two of his colleagues are openly giggling. One of the women isn't sharing the general hilarity, but isn't exactly protesting either. He goes on to add, 'I reckon I'd rather be queer than sleep with a nigger.'

Just for a moment, and even though I'm hardly what you'd call an expert on the subject, I'm wondering whether he's trying out some alternative comedy; but no – the man's sincere enough.

I look down at my watch. We'll be in Paris in a little under twenty minutes. I still have the other syringe that Chloé prepared. It's in my pocket. Why did she bother to make two of them anyway? I can feel it between my fingertips. It's ready to go. The temptation is strong. I hesitate for a few seconds longer but then get it out and slip it carefully up my sleeve. What happens next is up to him. If he goes for a pee, he's dead. If his bladder is as big as a bucket, he'll be allowed to carry on with his pathetic little existence – which would be a shame. I have high hopes. He's definitely the type to think about the practicalities of things. I can tell. He won't want to get a sudden urge when he's on the Métro or in a taxi.

The minutes go by and it doesn't look like anything's going to happen. I think about getting another beer because I need a reason to be hanging around here; I've been in the bar a while now. But then, I should be getting back to my stuff – particularly my mobile. They're looking down at their watches too, but the women both have their handbags already and the men their briefcases. I imagine they left nothing back at their seats.

Our train slows down and the first high-rises of the northern suburbs of Paris are coming into view. It's now or never.

'I'm dying to take a slash! Wait here for me.'

The sheer elegance of his words only serves to reassure me. My initial judgement was right. This man doesn't deserve to survive me. Why should I pass over to whatever comes next while he gets to stay here? He may well be around for decades to come. There's no rhyme nor reason and I need to remedy it.

He crosses the bar and steps into the toilets, which are situated at the far end of the adjacent carriage. I don't think he's the sort who washes his hands afterwards – I mean, everything else about him is disgusting. He won't be in there long. I'm standing in front of the door now. It just looks as though I'm waiting my turn. I've taken the needle from my sleeve and it's in my hand. I hear him flush the loo and the lock on the door opens within seconds. What did I say about hand-washing?

I have just enough time to pull off the little plastic tip at the end of the needle. A quick look left and then right. There's nobody in very close proximity. I slam the door into the bastard's head and push him with all my weight so that he's stuck behind it. He shouts out a little, but the sound is drowned out by the racket of the train slowing down. I add more pressure. I'm hurting him now. His left leg is totally jammed, and stretched out towards me. I stab the needle into his thigh, straight through his suit trousers.

I spot the first signs almost immediately. His body stiffens as he tries to let out whimpers of protest, but these soon turn into laboured breathing. There's no way he can even attempt to defend himself. I step away from the door a little. He is bathed in sweat and trying desperately to undo the knot in his tie. He doesn't manage it before his head bangs down into the stainless-steel washbasin.

I hope I can trust whatever it is I've just injected him with. Chloé did boast of its merits, but I could maybe have asked more questions. There's bound to be an autopsy and I hope that it establishes cardiac arrest as the cause of death.

I walk back in the direction I came and right past what has now become a trio. I overhear a snippet of their discussion which amuses me somewhat.

'Do you think his prostate is playing up?'

Spineless idiots. No sooner is his back turned than they . . . Well, I don't think they're going to miss their boss all that much.

When I get back to my seat, it's as if my high-maintenance neighbour is waiting for me to help her get her case back down. I pick up my papers and my phone and totally ignore her. I can sense that she isn't taking this too well. I think I actually hear her mutter something along the lines of 'That's nice', but I'm completely impervious. If she had any inkling as to what I've just done, she'd be a little more careful right now.

As I alight the train at Gare du Nord and cross the main hall with a spring in my step, I know I've done what needed to be done. In fact,

I believe this little stunt has done me some good. The shiver that went down my spine as I stuck the needle in and watched him keel over was really something. It truly is the simplest of pleasures and one I regret not having more time to repeat regularly. The only thing I'm a little concerned about is working out what to say to Chloé when she asks me for the second syringe back. Oh, I'll improvise. I'm more than capable of justifying my actions if it comes to it.

Actually, this all feels quite refreshing. I'm not in the same mood at all as when I left Lille. I prove this by not thinking twice about rubbing shoulders with the hoi polloi and getting on the Métro to make my way home.

When I exit Saint-Sulpice station, I feel as though all the Parisians have upped and left during my absence. It's a warm evening and I walk up Rue Bonaparte until I reach my flat. As I meander along, I'm overtaken by a few joggers who are building up a sweat around the streets of the Luxembourg district, but it's nowhere near as crowded as usual. I arrive outside the heavy door that leads to the indoor courtyard and type in the code, which lets me through to the entranceway and all the letterboxes. I open mine up, not expecting to find anything other than the odd bill. Wrong. There's some sort of official-looking envelope with a seal, but no stamp. I rip it open with my stomach churning. The letterhead reads *National Police Headquarters* and I'm immediately shaken. It's an appearance notice. I have to go and see a certain Major Charvin on Monday for 'an affair that concerns me'. This is going to ruin my entire evening.

CHAPTER 18

It's a long evening indeed. Very long. I pass a restless night, alternating between periods of sleep and interminable periods of insomnia, despite the sleeping tablet I take. At around 6 a.m., I finally accept that I'm not going to drift off again, so I get up and wait until I can call this Major Charvin. I get through to the station at 8 a.m. I'm told that he won't be there for at least another hour, but that a message will be passed on to him and that he'll be back in touch at his earliest convenience. It turns out that that's five minutes later. The fact that he calls me so soon makes me fear the worst.

His voice is, however, fairly reassuring. 'Monsieur Gaudin, first of all let me thank you for contacting me so quickly. It saves us both having to waste time waiting until Monday, doesn't it?'

'You're m-more than welcome,' I stammer.

'You don't live far from our offices, I believe. Would it bother you to pop over and see me this morning? If you're free, of course.'

'That's no problem at all. What time would suit?'

'Whenever is best for you. Now, if you like.'

'Yes, I can do that.'

'Righty ho, then. You need to come to 36 Quai des Orfèvres and tell my colleague on reception that you have a meeting with Major Charvin from the crime unit. You'll need a piece of ID.'

'Understood. But . . .'

'Yes?'

'Can you tell me what all this is about, please?'

'I'd rather explain everything face to face, but don't worry – it's probably all just a formality. See you shortly.'

I hang up, feeling just a little bit better.

◆ ◆ ◆

The police officer at the entrance to the building is very young. He has a way of looking at my ID card that makes me imagine what my face looks like when people go on at me for not eating organic food. He holds it between his thumb and forefinger and taps it on the desk while he uses his other hand to phone Charvin.

'Major? It's Berthoud down at the desk. I've got a Monsieur Gaudin who says you're expecting him.'

I can't hear the reply.

'That's fine. I'll send him up.'

He puts my ID card into a pigeonhole and explains, 'You need to take off anything metallic you have on you: keys, telephone, change . . . and then walk through the detector. Then cross the hallway. At the back, on the left, take the big staircase up to the second floor and someone will come and collect you. When you've finished, don't forget to come back and pick up your ID card. All sound good?'

'Err, yes . . . I think so.'

It's an intimidating place. I don't think I've ever even picked up a crime novel or watched *Poirot* on TV or anything like that, but there's something fascinating about 36 Quai des Orfèvres. The old stone walls, the inner courtyard, the monumental staircase with its worn-looking black lino . . . There's a solemn air throughout the building, not to mention the plain-clothes police whose mere presence is very imposing. I really hope that I'm not expected to be here long.

There's another reception desk of sorts at the top of the staircase. I start to approach it when I hear my name being called out.

'Monsieur Gaudin?'

He's plump with balding white hair and I imagine he can't be far off retiring. He's wearing jeans and a grey tailored jacket over a white shirt, but no tie. I notice a huge signet ring on his right hand. In my heightened state, I start imagining how much it would hurt if he were to give me a beating . . .

'That's me.'

'Major Charvin. Come with me.'

He unlocks a barrier and I walk through with him. Once we're on the other side, he turns back towards me and shakes my hand. The smile he gives me is bordering on warm.

'Thank you for coming to see me. Follow me. We'll chat in my office.'

I walk behind him as we make our way up an open staircase to the fourth floor and then down a labyrinth of narrow corridors leading to cramped offices. As I look up at the ceiling, I see dozens and dozens of uncovered electric cables smothered in years' worth of dust. The walls are yellowing and it's all pretty bleak. For such a prestigious address, I'm genuinely taken aback at its state of disrepair.

The major looks over his shoulder as he speaks. No doubt he's used to receiving people here and having to explain the condition of the building. 'People are always a little shocked when they first come to see us here. You wouldn't think that this is where some of the best police officers in France work, would you? I'm not talking about myself, of course. We're supposed to be moving in a few months.'

We arrive at a doorway. He pushes down on an old copper handle, the likes of which I haven't seen since I was knee-high.

'Come on in and sit down. My desk is just there on the right.'

The floor has a slight gradient and the space is poorly lit by a minuscule window up towards the ceiling. There are two other desks in the room, but neither is occupied. I take a seat, as requested, in front of the one on the right. The major walks behind it and sinks down with a sigh. He switches on one of those flexible desk lamps. I'm half expecting him to shine it in my eyes, but he turns it towards a pile of folders on his desk before taking the top one and opening it up.

'Monsieur Gaudin,' he begins, with kindness in his voice, 'we're currently looking into the worrying disappearance of someone and I have a few questions to ask you. I hope that's all right?'

Disappearance? So he doesn't want to see me about Reimbach, then. Maybe Stéphanie Tisserand? But that would mean her body hasn't yet been discovered. That'd be a bit of good luck for me.

'Of course it is . . .' I say falteringly. 'I'm all ears.'

He gets out a sheet of paper from the folder and studies it before showing it to me.

'Could you please confirm that since the twenty-seventh of June you've been in possession of a rented Renault Twingo with the registration plate CE 247 BR, and that you got this vehicle from the Hertz agency at Paris-Montparnasse?'

So, it *is* about Stéphanie Tisserand. I've been spotted.

Keep your cool, Régis, and think about what questions might crop up next.

'Yes, that's right. I'm renting a Twingo at the moment from Hertz. I'm not sure about the registration, though. It must be what you've said.'

'Very good. And you live at 4 Rue Guynemer in Paris. Is that information still correct?'

'Yes.'

'Can you tell me what you do for a living?'

'I'm an astrophysicist. I work for the National Scientific Research Centre. And I teach at the Institute of Astrophysics in Paris. But . . .'

'Yes?'

'I'm not really working there very much these days. I'm on sick leave for . . .' I allow a moment of silence to pass for him to take note of just how hard I'm finding it to accept my painful and delicate situation. '. . . cancer.'

He has the same reaction that everyone has when you tell them you've got cancer. He looks at me with compassion, blushes a little and makes nervous hand gestures. He is embarrassed.

'I'm sorry to hear that . . . I hope that . . . I hope that everything works out for you.'

I am tempted to say that it won't. Everything won't work out. I'm on borrowed time. But I don't want to get into all that, so I just give the standard reply. 'Everything that can be done is being done. We'll see how it all turns out. Please go ahead and ask your questions. My illness makes no difference to anything.'

I can tell he wants to congratulate me or even thank me for my courage, but he doesn't. He carries on with his interrogation in an increasingly professional manner.

'Very well. It seems that the vehicle you've hired has been seen parked close to where the missing person lives. It's been seen a lot, in fact. So that's why we're interested in the car . . . and the driver, of course.'

Think, Régis. Don't mess this up. 'Yes . . . That's possible. Perhaps he or she lives near me?'

'No, not at all. She lives in the sixteenth arrondissement.'

'The sixteenth?'

Take your time, Régis. No need to rush this. Whatever you say has to ring true.

'No, I don't know why my car would . . . Except . . . Of course! I'm so stupid.'

'Something come back to you?'

'Yes. I'm ever so sorry. I didn't put two and two together at first. I go for a walk every morning around the tracks at Auteuil. It's something I started doing when I was signed off work. At first, I just went around the Jardin du Luxembourg because I live just opposite it, but I got bored of the same old thing day in, day out. So then I changed it and started going to the Bois de Boulogne. Sorry for not even making the connection, but I forgot that Auteuil is in the sixteenth. I thought it counted as the suburbs.'

'No worries. How long have you been taking your constitutional around there, then?'

'I'd say . . . about three or four weeks?'

'And do you always park in the same spot?'

'Yeah, I do. I park on a road down by the racing track, you know? I couldn't tell you the name. But there's always room and it's free parking down there. That's the only reason I go there.'

He seems satisfied with my answer, but then he looks down at his notes and his brow furrows.

'Three or four weeks, you say?'

'Around that, yes.'

'But you didn't hire the car all that long ago, did you? Did you have another one before that?'

Don't panic. The answer has to sound natural. 'No. I took public transport before that. But it was taking an age to get anywhere, and my doctor told me I shouldn't be staying cooped up at home. So I thought renting a car might be a good solution. It motivates me to get out and about more.'

'I see.'

He doesn't see at all, but the important thing is that it looks like he's believing every word that's falling out of my mouth, and that's all I'm bothered about. But I mustn't congratulate myself too soon because it looks like he has more questions for me. He's taking his time, though. Is it because of the state of my health? I suppose even a copper might have scruples when it comes to harassing people with cancer.

He proves my point as he smiles and states reassuringly, 'I knew you'd be able to clear everything up and that it'd be nothing but a coincidence. I'll be letting you get on your way now to . . .'

He lets the sentence hang in mid-air. He hasn't quite finished with me, though. I know it.

'I have one more thing to ask you . . .'

What did I say?

'Have your professional activities, or even your personal ones for that matter, ever led you to cross paths with an agency called Pearl Events? They supply hostesses and the like.'

Her company. Watch yourself, Régis. Don't blow it. You need to play the innocent here. 'Hostesses? An agency for hostesses? By that, I suppose you mean . . . ? Do you . . . do you mean escort people? Like prostitute girls?'

He holds it in, but I can see he wants to laugh. 'No,' he says, doing his best to suppress his chuckles. 'It's nothing like that. It's just the young women and men you see at conferences and exhibitions and such. They welcome visitors, hand out drinks . . .'

'I see . . .' I stay focused on my role of man who is totally out of touch with reality. I'm amazed at how good I am at it. 'No. I don't think I've ever heard of them. You know, in astrophysics, we don't tend to get out of the lab much.'

'That's what I thought,' he says.

He's going to let me go any minute now. I can feel it. I just have to make sure I act normal on the way out. Should I leave without asking any further questions? Would it be suspicious to be too curious? What would someone who had nothing to do with the whole business actually say in a situation like this? I think it would be unusual to be interrogated by a police officer and then not be in the slightest bit interested as to what was going on. He is already standing up and gives me the nod, so I do the same.

OK. I'm going in.

'Can I ask you something?'

He stops and puts both hands on his hips. He's smiling quite broadly at this point. 'Ask anything you like. I can't promise you I'll answer, though.'

We both sit back down, and he gestures for me to continue speaking.

'I was just wondering . . . You know the person who has disappeared . . . Was it someone important?'

He wasn't expecting this. In fact, he looks very surprised by my question. He thinks for a while. I don't imagine he's wondering whether or not to answer, but rather whether Stéphanie Tisserand was someone you'd call 'important'.

'No,' he ends up saying. 'She's your average woman. "Ordinary", I'd say. She has her own business and lives quite comfortably, but no more than that.'

Wow. I wait for him to tell me more. He doesn't. He shifts in his chair a little. I was too curious.

'And why do you ask such a question?'

On your guard now, Régis. No slip-ups. 'Huh? Oh . . . no reason. I just wondered. I once saw a documentary on the police who work here and I thought you only dealt with cases involving proper VIPs. That's all. So I was just being nosy. I thought it might be a famous person.'

That was a good answer. He stands up again and he's openly laughing now. 'Not at all. We deal with all cases. Anything that's required of us. Whether it's the exciting celebrity cases or Joe Bloggs. The person we're looking for is someone just like you and me.'

Someone just like you and me. They don't know what Stéphanie Tisserand was up to, then. Maybe it's too soon for them to have worked it all out.

Chapter 19

I meet up with Chloé six days later. I suppose she's been in Paris since Friday, Saturday at the latest, but I think she didn't want to show her face until I'd had my treatment and the side effects had worn off. I ask her what she's been doing with her time, but it's a total waste of breath as she has no answers to give me. I don't bother letting her in on what's happened to me since I last saw her. Not a word about the incident on the train and even less about what took place at 36 Quai des Orfèvres. I settle for telling her about Lazreg's visit instead. He found me on good form last week. I don't think anything will change in the grand scheme of things, but he seemed optimistic about it all.

Chloé has taken me out on a field trip in preparation for our next hit. We're in one of the dodgier suburbs, I'd say. It's certainly not somewhere I've ever visited regularly, and I would never have thought that what happens right now before our very eyes could actually occur in real life; even though I've never been one to follow the TV news, I've always been convinced that production teams add a little extra excitement here and there to get audiences hooked.

A BMW coupé skids on its back wheels, flips up into the air, turns on its roof and comes to a stop in a cloud of thick black smoke. Further back, two sports cars rev their engines before hurtling off at great speed and smashing into a wall about a hundred metres away. On purpose. A new car enters the fracas, almost banging into both cars from behind, its brakes screeching and practically deafening us. It's a huge 4x4 with disproportionately large wheels, multicoloured tube lighting underneath and a huge bull bar at the front covered in headlamps. I've never seen anything like it. Perhaps it's the sort of truck you might need on a night-time safari, but I can't see much use for it in the Paris suburbs.

I quickly work out that discretion isn't something these hothead boy-racers hold dear. Even the youngest among them, those far too young to have driving licences, are performing acrobatics and skids on their scooters or handbrake turns on their mini quad bikes.

We watch them from a safe distance, sheltering behind some bushes that separate the dual carriageway from the supermarket car park.

'They won't stay around for long,' Chloé, who's driven us out here, assures me.

'Do you come here often?'

'Sometimes. And it's always the same scenario. They wait until the police show up, just for the hell of it. I think the thrill is in the chase. They give them the finger and off they go in different directions. Then they all meet up in some other car park they've agreed on in advance, and it starts again. They carry on like that until dawn.'

'And are we going to follow them all night?'

'If that's your thing, then go ahead – but I won't be coming with you.'

We remain silent for a few seconds in the middle of the screeching horns and blaring sound systems. Then a small group starts to form in the centre of the car park. There are around fifteen baseball-capped youths all surrounding an older-looking lad who stands head and shoulders above the lot of them.

My intuition comes into play.

'Is he there?' I ask Chloé, without having to spell out my thoughts.

'Damn straight he is. And I reckon you've already spotted him.'

As much as the distance between us will allow, I pick out the one I assume is the leader of the gang, the guy Chloé started telling me about on our trip out here. He's black, tall, stocky . . . Actually, I'd call him fat. He's wearing a blue satin jacket and a yellow bandana over his shaved head – at least, I imagine it's shaved. Even though it's almost pitch-black apart from the car headlights, he's wearing sunglasses. There's also a large gold medallion that hits him in the chest every time he moves. He's chewing gum non-stop and his presence seems to dominate. He has a team of people surrounding him. They're there to protect him, but they keep their distance. It's probably a mark of respect or something.

'That big black guy dressed up like a clown?'

'Got it in one, Régis. It's my honour to introduce you to Abdou Nkomo.'

'He looks a right charmer. Quite the colourful character, eh? What can you tell me about him?'

'He's a notorious dealer. That's his main job, but he has no problem with violent robberies or racketeering either. He's been behind bars more than once, but every time he's released he just comes out a bit better at what he does. All the kids around where he lives want to work for him. He uses them as mules or he sticks them down in the Métro to pickpocket the tourists. He's a real dick.'

I don't like bad-mouthing people I don't know, but I have to say that this man looks every inch the bad guy. Not only in terms of his physique and wardrobe choices, but also in his attitude towards the young kids around him. It looks like he's giving some of them grief and scaring others off with his jeers or a couple of smacks around the head. With a chosen few, however, he's cool. He's giving them high-fives or quick, tight hugs with slaps on the back. He's the boss. Every single one of his gestures confirms as much.

As we continue to watch, I notice another individual show up. He's younger than Abdou. He looks to be of North African origin and he follows the same dress code as the rest of them: a white T-shirt, hoodie and eye-catchingly bright trainers. The boss has also seen him arrive and has his eyes fixed on him. From where I am, I can't hear a word, but I don't believe this young man has said anything yet. I don't think anyone has uttered a syllable, in fact. Instinctively, the rest of the gang seems to part ways and hang back to make room for this guy. Abdou Nkomo advances to meet him and, hands in pockets, confirms his scorn for him by spitting on the ground. Once they're directly facing one another, Abdou is more than a head taller than the newcomer. He removes his hands from his pockets and places them abruptly around the kid's neck. He then runs with him for a few yards and bangs him up against a car, placing two fingers between his eyes to mimic a gun. He mutters something in his face, but we'll never know what that was. Two cars with blue flashing lights make a sudden appearance at the far end of the car park. Just as quickly, everyone in sight rushes into their cars or on to scooters and scrambles out of there. My new target reacts in the same way. He's gone. He lets go of his prey and jumps into an Audi. I only know the make because I manage to catch a glimpse of the badge on the back. He's not driving. This man has a chauffeur, if you please! I know it's far from being the fastest car in the world, but within seconds all I can see of it are a couple of twinkling lights in the distance. The police are out of their vehicles and all six of them pile on to some poor devil whose scooter won't start. The show's over for tonight. We find Chloé's car again and start making our way back to Paris.

As soon as we're on the A86, she leans across and gets out the customary envelope from the glove compartment. It's a lot heftier than any that have come before. As well as photos of the man himself taken from every angle, there are pictures of a young black girl – very pretty, but dressed in a way that leaves little to the imagination, and with the sort of make-up I find quite vulgar. But, each to their own. There are also two addresses. His, in Orly. And hers, in Villeneuve-Saint-Georges. I also have a couple of maps which mean nothing to me, and a wad of €100 notes. If I had to take a wild guess, I'd say there was €3–4,000 in total. Easily. I put off taking a more in-depth look at the contents and close up the envelope before placing it on the dashboard.

Without taking her eyes off the road, Chloé smirks slightly as she asks, 'No questions?'

'Yes! And I've no doubt you've got all the answers.'

We're just reaching the A4 now. At this hour, if we take the road that follows the river we can get to mine in less than fifteen minutes.

Chloé must be thinking the same thing as she yawns and looks down at her watch. 'OK. I'll be quick about it and we'll go into everything in greater detail tomorrow. Is that OK with you?'

'Yes. You know I'm at your service. As always.'

She slaps my thigh – mocking me, I believe. I'm sure it's wishful thinking, but I get the impression that her hand may have rested longer than necessary on my leg. But I don't manage to dwell on such thoughts before my boss gets back to business.

'The money in there is just for some expenses. We're sure you're out of pocket on what we've asked you to do so far.'

'If you say so.'

'That's right!' She laughs. 'I do say so!'

She then becomes serious and turns to me very briefly. 'Régis, you've seen who you're going to be dealing with and I'm sure you understand that you'll have to tread very carefully.' She looks back to the road, thankfully, but keeps talking. 'There's no way you can just go with the flow and act on instinct again. You just won't get away with it.'

She's not kidding. That man must be at least thirty kilos heavier than me, for a start. And I can't imagine him going off for a stroll in the woods on his own either. I bet he never goes anywhere without at least two or three big roughnecks with him. This will be no mean feat. I tell Chloé my worries and she agrees with me as we pass under the Bercy bridge.

'Yes. You've seen him. The photo of the young woman in the envelope is his girlfriend. He sleeps over at her place two or three times a week. Her name is Farisa Goumi. We don't have all that much on her. She doesn't seem to have a job. We believe that she's his "official" partner, but it doesn't stop him having the occasional liaison with some of his female clients or women he meets in nightclubs. He likes to get them drunk on champagne. It's more than occasional, actually. He's not exactly the faithful type.'

I'm starting to get a pretty clear picture of the guy, and I'm coming to the conclusion that, when the moment arrives, I won't have any trouble putting an end to this one. I'm making progress. I'm really coming into my own. I reflect again on what a shame it is that such a promising career is about to be curtailed.

'So what's the plan?' I ask, batting these thoughts to one side.

'There isn't much of one, really. As I said, he's extremely careful. There's some consolation, though – we've managed to hack his email, but he only uses it for humdrum stuff. I've put the password in the envelope for you. See if you can get anything out of it. He does most of his drug dealing on huge estates. There are two of them – Orly and Choisy-le-Roi. Where the high-rises are, you know? I've given you two maps. That's where he is most of the time. But you have to be really careful. You're going to have to study this one. From seven in the evening until five the next morning, his gang is in full control of who goes in and out of all those blocks. It could all get messy very quickly if anyone sees you. We're going to have your back, just in case.'

'Oh, so I have a few more long days ahead of me. Or nights, in this instance.'

'I'll try to be more available to you this time. Promise. I can take over when you're tired.'

I take this as good news, even though I'd prefer it if she didn't take over at all. I'd rather she was just with me. I don't much fancy the thought of her being parked in a car on her own in the middle of some nightmare of an estate. God only knows what these people would be capable of if they got hold of her.

As we arrive at Austerlitz, we find ourselves driving slowly behind a bus. There's a huge advert on the back for a rap concert. The 'singer', if that's what you'd call him, has the exact same look as our Abdou Nkomo. Behind him are two pin-up girls with huge fake bosoms, each brandishing a revolver provocatively. The image prompts a question that I haven't yet asked myself. It falls from my lips as soon as it enters my mind.

'Why him?'

'What?'

I point to the ad on the back of the bus. 'There are men like him all over the place! Even if this guy is a massive drug dealer or trafficker or whatever you want to call it, I doubt he has the monopoly on drug sales throughout France. Even Paris! There'll be someone like him on every estate, in every suburb, in every city. So why this one?'

For the first time, I feel like I've asked a daft question. Chloé looks at the back of the bus and her lips curl.

'What are you on about! It's nothing to do with *him*! He's an amazing artist!' she cries.

'I know that, but you know what I mean. All you've got to do is head down to Fresnes or Fleury-Mérogis and you'll see dealers coming in and out of the flats all day long. So why this Abdou Nkomo? What's so special about him?'

As we continue up Rue Saint-Jacques, Chloé remains silent for a while. Just as we reach Place de l'Odéon, she lets out a long sigh and, as she does so, I know I should be able to trust her. This guy must be a real piece of shit if we're even talking about doing what we're going to do. She doesn't utter another word until we're outside my building.

'Are you seeing your doctor again soon?'

'Yes. In three days.'

'Right. I suggest meeting after that and we can talk it all through.'

Is she stonewalling me? I don't insist on getting my explanation. It really doesn't look like there's one coming anyway. I step out of the car and slam the door behind me. She starts the engine again and she's off in the blink of an eye. So much for my feelings.

I feel stuck between two thoughts. I'm sad that she isn't paying a little more attention to me – romantically speaking. But then that's always been the case. And I'm worried that she doesn't seem to want to answer my question at all.

CHAPTER 20

Professor Lazreg comes to administer my treatment. I start by getting him a glass of water and opening a beer for myself.

Our conversation centres on what's been happening in the news. An attack on a refugee centre has just been thwarted and my doctor is talking ten to the dozen about the intolerance and selfishness of our society. There's also a Jewish children's holiday camp that was attacked by a group of Islamic teenagers not much older than the kids in the place. Fanatics, we're told. The doctor goes into a new spiel now about the radicalisation of young Muslims in the suburbs of Paris. I have to admit, I'm finding it hard to engage with all this. I'm just not that interested. It's not that I'm insensitive to children's suffering. At least, I don't think I am. It's just that I know that, however hard I try, I'll never be able to understand why anyone could think that seventy-two virgins might be waiting for them in paradise, or that Jewish children should only go on holiday with other Jewish children, or that if on Sunday you take a sip of wine and a bite of bread that you're taking the flesh and blood of an Aramaic chap who died two thousand years ago. I just don't get any of it. I've spent the best part of my life studying the birth of matter and the formation of the universe. I think that if there had been some divine intervention in any of it then I, or one of my esteemed colleagues, would have seen traces of it. And I don't believe I'll be changing my mind on the matter any time soon.

'We're going to be doing a few more tests.'

He springs it on me – just like that.

'Do you really think I need more of that right now?'

He gives me the annoyed frown of an eminent doctor whose decisions are being questioned. But he knows how to deal with people like me and has an answer for me within seconds. 'I can see that you're handling your treatment remarkably well. You're resisting the disease. But there are no miracles, as well you know. You must also understand that I am doing my very best to make sure you suffer as little as possible. And these tests will help me to do just that.'

'In that case . . .'

◆ ◆ ◆

Scans, X-rays, blood tests, urine samples, stool samples . . . I spend a whole day at the hospital and am now going to collect the results.

When I get there, there are only two people in Lazreg's waiting room. A woman in her mid-sixties who has just come in for a check-up. More than likely, her GP has sent her in for tests just to get her to stop bugging him, because it's evident to me that she's never lived with the darkness of a malignant tumour. There's also a man. He's a little younger. Probably fifty. He's done for. You can just see it. He carries it with him. Perhaps he's not even aware of it himself yet. They might not have given him the news, but I would bet what little life I have left that he's no better off than me. I don't know how I can be so certain of such things, but I am convinced of my diagnoses. I don't enjoy this new-found gift of mine. It's not a power I'd wish on anyone, but I wonder if it's something you develop once you're condemned to death. A kind of sixth sense. Perhaps he'll discover he has it, too.

Half an hour later, they've both gone to their different destinities and I know that it'll be my turn any minute now.

'Hello, Monsieur Gaudin.'

I didn't hear him arrive in the waiting room. He holds the door ajar with his foot and offers me his hand to shake. He seems in a much better mood than usual. He's warmer somehow. I join him in his office and sit down in the chair facing his desk. Same old, same old. I've done it a hundred times. But Lazreg has an amused smile on his face as he watches me. Before he takes a seat himself, I ask him why he's so cheerful.

'No reason,' he says, sounding apologetic. 'It's a little strange to see you here in such professional surroundings. I'm no longer used to it.'

I understand perfectly what he means. This visit is having an odd effect on me, too. He's been coming to my flat, having his glasses of water, discussing all sorts of topics other than my illness, and although I wouldn't exactly say we were friends, we have reached a certain level of intimacy; and now we both feel out of place in his sterile office.

'Let me tell you where we're at.' As soon as his backside hits his chair he's opening up my file on his computer. 'Hmm . . . Obviously . . .'

He doesn't seem happy about something, but I don't think I've done or said anything that might displease him. He hasn't really ever told me anything about what changes I should be making to my diet or anything like that. And I don't have any medication to take other than what he administers himself. So what can I have done wrong? I'd better find out.

'What's going on, Doctor?'

The voice and the tone I employ surprise me. I'm talking to him as if I doubt him somehow. But he's done nothing wrong. Do I only have two weeks left? Would that really change anything? He doesn't seem to notice my aggression. I don't think he's even heard me. He continues to read the results on the screen and mutters to himself inaudibly. I discreetly get my phone out of my pocket to check the time and decide that I'm only going to let him give me the silent treatment for a further two minutes. Then I'm going to really let him have it.

He remembers my existence just eleven seconds before the deadline.

'Monsieur Gaudin?'

'Yes.'

'I'm afraid I don't have good news for you.'

'Oh. You hoped there would be some?'

He seems hesitant. He always does when it's anything to do with my sickness. He throws his glasses down on to the desk. 'I didn't. But, to tell you the truth, the way you were reacting to the treatment made me think that perhaps we could slow down the process. But that's not the case at all. What I told you a few months ago still stands.'

'Which means?'

'Which means that in eight to ten weeks your treatment will no longer be considered worth pursuing. You will be hospitalised again, and it will all move very quickly after that.'

I take in what he's saying. It's definite. Concrete. I can see the last few hurdles quite clearly now.

'That's fine, Doctor.'

'I'll continue to treat you until we . . . get to that point,' he adds insistently. 'And I'll do everything in my power to ensure you remain as comfortable as possible.'

I suddenly feel very old and ill.

'Are you going to be OK?'

'Yes. Don't worry about me. I've reached a place of acceptance now. It's just the date . . .'

'We'll talk about it more next week. Unless . . . I think I can trust you, can't I?'

I don't know where he's going with a question like that, but I nod, feeling shy. 'I think so, Doctor.'

'It's just that . . . I told you that your treatment hasn't been approved in France . . . and that it would be difficult for anyone to treat you other than me.'

'I remember all that, of course.'

'And so I thought that if you wanted to make the most of the time . . . left . . . and if you think you could manage the injections yourself . . . I could perhaps give you enough for the next couple of weeks.'

I don't quite know what to say. I know that he must have thought about this for a long time before offering it to me as a possibility, and that I should thank him.

'That's very kind of you. I'll think about it.' We both stand and walk to the door, where I add, 'Of course, you can count on my discretion.'

Chapter 21

Prior to meeting Chloé, I'd been to a nightclub on just the one occasion in my forty-four years on this earth; now, this was my second time in a month. And what dreadful places they've proved to be! The club that just goes by the initial S, which she took me to for some hardcore training, gave me the fright of my life, but the Bronco is as nightmarish as they come. The music? Incomprehensible bellowing between loud squeaks and scratchy noises from the turntables. The décor? Well, the dimmed lights give me a (fortunately) reduced view of what's going on, but from what I can make out, the walls are plastered with naked girls in all sorts of compromising positions and very often with some sort of cooking utensil or piece of cleaning equipment in their hands . . . which they're using for pretty much anything but household chores. In perfect keeping with the place, the clientele seems semi-wild. They're screaming, scuffling and showing off like kids. I've never witnessed anything quite like it. Oh, and I forgot to mention . . . 99 per cent of the punters are black. So Chloé and I stick out like sore thumbs as we make our way through the crowds. It's a miracle the bouncers even let us enter. But now we're sitting on a red velvet bench, trying to blend in . . . or at least not be noticed. Neither of us take our eyes off the entrance. And even though my age and attire suggest I'm the odd one out in the place, Chloé's the one suffering as she sits by my side. It's the first time

I've seen her lose both her optimism and her good humour simultaneously. I think that she feels guilty, too – because the reason we're here is that Nkomo slipped through our fingers this afternoon. I wasn't there; she'd insisted I stay at home and rest a little. The way it happened was ridiculous, as these things always are. He'd disappeared into the bowels of the estate just as business was starting to boom out in the car park. A police car turned up and patrolled the area. Nothing out of the ordinary there. The police drive round these estates every day putting up with insults and jibes from the youths who hang out in front of the tower blocks. It's just that today, as they finished their tour, they were joined by six other riot vans which all took position in front of the high-rises. Everyone scarpered: every man for himself. And Nkomo was no exception. Chloé didn't catch sight of him again. No doubt the subterranean levels of the place are full of escape exits and he was out of there like a rat out of a sewer.

Chloé did her best to find him by going through the usual channels: local dives, the homes of his closest friends and allies, his regular clients . . . but there was neither hide nor hair of him. She headed back towards his neighbourhood, the Navigateurs estate, and, with extreme caution, went down to the basement level, where there was a vast underground system of garages and storage spaces. She couldn't find his Audi R8, which is usually parked down there and guarded by one of his lackeys. It was at this point that she decided to call me.

I wasn't in particularly good shape when the phone rang. She must have guessed this by the sound of my voice because, when I offered to join her, she refused outright. But I am finding it harder and harder to deal with the insomnia I've recently started to suffer from, and couldn't rest as she'd asked; so I managed to convince her to come and pick me up so that we could seek him out as a team.

This is how we ended up in the hell that is the Bronco. By now, we're both starting to get a little on the desperate side. We know that this is the only place we have any chance of finding him at 3 a.m. We know he comes here a lot. But neither of us has ever actually crossed the threshold before. We usually just follow him as far as the car park, watch him go inside and then know that nothing of much interest is going to happen until the following day. But we decide to venture inside tonight, in the hope (the absurd hope) that we might pick up a few clues on how to establish contact with the man.

'We shouldn't have bothered coming! We're never going to get anywhere!'

She screams this in my ear, but I only just catch what she's saying. At least there's no chance of anyone overhearing our conversation if even I can't hear her over the din.

'Why? Do you think he won't bother showing?'

'I don't think so. And if he does turn up, he's going to spot us straight away, isn't he? We don't exactly blend in.'

I can't say she's wrong about that. Quite a few people have been giving us odd looks. They've been paying particular attention to Chloé and . . . to her curves, I imagine. The men in here aren't exactly the subtle type. They look at me immediately afterwards and must be asking themselves, and I'm getting quite used to this by now, *what's she doing with a bloke like that?*

'What do you suggest, then?'

'I don't know.'

She spits this last sentence out nastily. It's not like her, but I understand her frustration. We've been following him for eight days now. We've been either working together or taking it in turns to try not to let this Nkomo out of our sights. We have to break off sometimes, though, usually between 3 and 10 a.m. We now have a good idea of the sorts of things he gets up to during the day: examples include the delivery at a motorway service station car park of a significant number of suspect packages, several pick-ups of cash from his various dealers, and a bit of a punch-up with one of his bodyguards after some sort of disagreement.

I even watched, from afar, what looked like a territory negotiation with another of the big bosses from one of the estates on the eastern side of Paris. Chloé has told me quite a lot about his private life, too. His sex life, in any case. This man is a sex addict and a pervert, it seems. He enjoys using his power over women to satisfy his carnal instincts. There are quite a lot of cash-strapped junkies out there who'll do anything for a fix. But it's not only them. He also sleeps with the girlfriends of his fellow gang members. He somehow has that right. And then, of course, there's the odd lady of the night here and there who he enjoys time with in the back of his car or in bar toilets. He's certainly given us plenty to do. We're never bored when we're watching him, but we always go home feeling rather nauseated. And it's all been for nothing.

We can't find a flaw in his system. He is armed. Always. He is dangerous. He is never alone. When he sleeps, there are two or three of his henchmen parked in a car outside his flat. There's even one inside the flat itself. Or outside the front door if he's enjoying some time with his girlfriend. This is going to be complicated, no two ways about it.

All this must be contributing to the fact that I haven't been able to sleep much recently. I've spent so many hours watching this man and when I find myself alone I spend even more time wondering how we're ever going to get near him. When Chloé takes over from me and tells me to go home and take it easy, I can only stay in front of the television for a few minutes before I start pacing up and down, trying to work out a solution, trying to find the chink in his armour that will allow us to operate in safety. But nothing comes to me.

It's ludicrous. I know that's what most people would think. From where I stand right now, I might as well head off on a kamikaze mission and take him out in the middle of the street. With a little bit of luck, I might just escape his gang . . . but I'd be more likely to get a bullet in my brain and that'd be the end of that. At least I'd avoid being hunted down in a revenge killing. I'd also miss out on the agony that's probably awaiting me in a hospital bed.

'We'd better just go. I'm not feeling it.'

Chloé declares her decision and hops straight to her feet, ready to make a quick exit. I also feel the need to get the hell out of here, but at the same time I have my doubts. A voice inside my head is urging me to stay – saying that if we do we'll learn something important. But I know Chloé well by now and I know there'll be no stopping her, so I stand up to follow.

It is at this moment that the DJ chooses to change the tune. He's doing some sort of loop thing with the records. It means that for a few moments – not long – the volume of the music lowers enough for us to pick up on a snippet of a conversation taking place between a client and the barman.

' . . . need to see Abdou. Is he here?'

'No. And you won't see him for some time. Fari told me he's gone to ground for a while. I don't know where he is. He took a plane out of here this afternoon anyway. He thinks he . . .'

Abdou . . . It can only be our Abdou Nkomo. Fari must be a nickname for his girlfriend. Farisa Goumi. Chloé can't help herself. She stops in her tracks. The barman stares at us and I push her forward a bit so that he doesn't get a good look at our faces. We walk to the exit under the suspicious eyes of the young woman working in the cloakroom and the bouncer on the door. When we get to the car park, Chloé stops again. I try to nudge her towards the car. There are too many people around and I don't imagine they'd necessarily take our side in the event of a scuffle. I get behind the wheel ready to drive us out of the danger zone and she climbs in beside me, but I haven't even started up the engine before she starts protesting.

'Don't, Régis! We need to go back.'

'No way! It's too dangerous!'

'We'll go about it carefully! Just leave it to me! I can get the barman to believe that . . .'

'You've no chance! What's got into you? You'll only have to say a couple of words and Nkomo will be warned that some dodgy woman is looking for him.'

'*Dodgy!* Thanks a lot!'

'You know what I mean. You're not the type he usually hangs out with.'

'But we need to know where he's gone. I'm sure this is our only chance.'

'I totally agree with you. If he's gone off on his travels, he'll be a lot less protected than he is at home. A lot less careful, too. And he's not the sort of person to go unnoticed. We'd stand a better chance of putting him down abroad.'

'But we need to know exactly where he's hiding out and how long he's planning on staying there.'

'We can find out. It's just that there are more discreet ways of doing things.'

'Care to let me in on them?'

'I will. In twenty minutes. That's how long it'll take us to get back to Paris. And in the future, remember that I was the one who had some sense here tonight.'

◆ ◆ ◆

I leave Chloé in my living room warming her hands on a cup of tea, in the hope that the caffeine will be enough to keep her awake. I also switch on the TV. Some 1980s sitcom is playing. I head through to my office and close the door behind me. I need to spend some time alone on the old Web. I give myself fifteen minutes, but just ten minutes later I'm able to go and fetch Chloé to come and take a look.

Contrary to expectations, she's wide awake. I'm actually surprised to find her laughing her head off in front of my huge flat-screen. She turns and looks at me as I enter the room, unable to contain her giggles.

'I didn't even know this was still on! I've always loved it! I never missed an episode when I was at school.'

'Well, now you know what to do with yourself when we're done. Are you coming? I've found him.'

She hardly reacts to the news I've just given her. She stands but pauses in front of the television for a couple more seconds, trying to catch another gag before switching it off and following me through to my office.

She leans in to look at my screen and I get the reaction I was hoping for.

'What? "*IBIZA. Return. 24 JULY . . .*" What is this site? Honestly, I can truly say I'm gobsmacked!'

Her eyes are glued to the screen, on which appears Nkomo's parking reservation.

'It's a confirmation email for his car. He wants it under lock and key.'

'And how come you thought of that?'

'Easy! You know how much care he takes of that thing. There's no way he'd leave it in your average airport car park. He'd want it in a private facility. Tucked away nice and safe. Somewhere with a taxi service to the airport. There are only two places that offer that kind of thing and they're both near Roissy. And when you make a booking with them, you need to give them your return flight number. You gave me the password for his account. All I had to do was open his mailbox and it all fell into place.'

'You're just fabulous!' She doesn't give me enough time to savour my moment of triumph before she's on to the next part of the plan. 'So, the twenty-fourth of July! That gives us ten days. So tomorrow, or worst-case scenario, the day after tomorrow . . .'

'Don't forget that we're slap-bang in the middle of the school holidays.'

'I can still manage it. It's just a matter of price, isn't it? And what's great is that Ibiza isn't that big a place. And, like you said, he's hard to miss, but we'll have our work cut out if we want to know what hotel he's in.'

'I know where he's staying.'

I might be getting above my station, but I'm sure that she's more than impressed with me this time. I add modestly, 'The flight is managed by one of those tour operators specialising in all-inclusive clubbing holidays. It's not the sort of holiday I know a lot about, but basically, you pay for the flight and full board at a hotel and then you get a pass to go to all the clubs and drink your fill. I went on their site and I found the name of the hotel they've partnered up with. It's called Bora-Bora.'

Chloé seems to have rediscovered the enthusiasm that had deserted her back in the club. I know she's itching to get into my chair to take over.

'I need to take a look at flights,' she says, grabbing the mouse out of my hand.

She's already opened up three different flight comparison sites before she pauses, her head spinning back to look at me. She frowns.

'You had your last injection a couple of days ago, right? When have you got to see your doctor again?'

'Monday. I'm seeing him on Monday.'

'That means we're going to have to wait until Tuesday before we can leave. Or we go now, and you nip back quickly to see your doctor and then fly back over to join me. What do you think?'

'I'll call my doctor. I reckon I can sort it out with him. There's no need for all the to-ing and fro-ing. Just get whatever tickets you can for tomorrow evening.'

'Are you sure about this?'

'My doctor won't refuse me a thing. We're beyond that now.'

CHAPTER 22

I've jumped ahead of myself a little, though. Professor Lazreg has no problem at all with my request, but I'll have to wait until he gets back from a seminar in Montpellier and comes to my house on Saturday morning.

When he arrives, he has sorted it all out in advance and everything is ready for me in a little travel case. On the phone, I explained that I was hoping to go away for a week – ten days at the most – and that I'd only require a single dose of my treatment; but he ends up giving me two syringes and two vials, insisting that I could always stay away a little longer should the desire take me.

I can read between the lines easily enough. He means for me to live out the little time I have left as independently as possible, before I succumb to the inevitable weakening that awaits me, and my final days in a hospital bed. He gives me a very quick examination, which simply comprises taking my blood pressure and a quick feel around the glands in my throat. I don't think he even bothers to read the measurement. He is quite clearly going through the motions and not expecting to see the slightest improvement in my state.

He does, however, spend rather a lengthy amount of time briefing me on the precautions I need to take regarding the illegal injections I'm now in possession of. He starts by handing me a prescription which explains why I have these substances, so that I can get through airport security or a potential customs interview. He then, of course, reminds me again that he doesn't actually have the right to prescribe this drug and that, should I run into difficulties at any point, it's probably wise if I don't actually take the treatment, but rather call a doctor and ask that he or she make direct contact with him. He reiterates this point several times and I have to reassure him that I've understood.

Strangely, although he's always been more than interested in the comings and goings of my life, he doesn't ask a single question as to my destination. He's probably too worried about professional culpability. He leaves in a hurry and again makes a point of insisting that I can reach him at any time, day or night. I suppose this gives me a little comfort, although with the ultimate prognosis being what it is, nothing is really encouraging.

And on that subject, although I don't feel any of the symptoms he's warned me of, I have taken a definite step back from life in general. I'm no longer that interested in what's happening with the accelerator at CERN. I don't really have an iota of concern when it comes to what my colleagues have been up to, and I am finding it increasingly difficult to remain focused on what my students are doing. Rain Man has left the building.

Chloé is the first to notice this change in my behaviour. She is even more perceptive now than she was when I first met her. She worries constantly about my levels of fatigue and knows that I can't be expected to 'work' for long hours at a stretch. She's not the only one. My neighbours have also become aware of my situation. I've only exchanged a couple of words with some of them and I'm fairly sure I didn't say a thing about my illness. But we mustn't forget Madame Rodriguez, the concierge.

Back when there was hope and a taxi would come and pick me up twice a week to take me to the hospital, she grabbed me one day on my way back up to my flat. She 'bumped' into me in the entrance hall on the pretext that she had a very important letter to give me. I had to go into her little lodge on the ground floor and sit there and be questioned until I gave her every last detail of my suffering. A suffering that has only worsened. And so she must have shouted it from the rooftops. Well, maybe not quite . . . but she's certainly spilled the beans to the neighbours, because they've all been giving me these heartfelt looks that I can't stand. Until today, not one of them has ventured forth to ask me anything – because when you live in a bourgeois neighbourhood like mine, people are discreet and rarely venture more than a 'Good morning' or a 'Good evening'. On rare occasions they feel adventurous enough to attempt a 'How are you?'

But it's the former minister (and now doctor) who breaks with protocol and comes to speak to me. He is bold enough to come to the door – in a very professional manner, I might add – to let me know that he is in contact with people in his network and is trying to get me an appointment with a renowned specialist he knows. I thank him warmly, but insist that I feel I'm in very good hands with Lazreg, and that, although I wouldn't hesitate to consult his colleague should I feel the need, the opinion of a second doctor doesn't seem necessary . . . given my situation. He has a couple more words of encouragement to offer me, then leaves me to my sofa and television.

But he's not the only one who's intent on bothering me; and this time, it's somewhat harder to deal with. I get a call from our Major Charvin from the Quai des Orfèvres.

The phone rings very early in the morning, when I've had one of the worst nights' sleep in a while. He must pick up on this from my voice. In fact, even with my initial 'Hello' I sound as weak as a kitten.

He excuses himself with exaggerated politeness. 'Monsieur Gaudin, I most sincerely apologise for disturbing you at this ungodly hour. Please believe me that, given the state of your health, if it were in my power to spare you this, I would do so. But I'm afraid I'm going to have to ask that I see you again.'

'No apologies necessary,' I manage to muster in as cheerful a tone as I can. 'You're only doing your job. Do you need me to come in?'

'No. Listen, I'm already embarrassed at having to disturb you like this. Would it be at all possible for me to pop over and see you? I won't be long.'

'If you want. Just give me half an hour.'

Exactly thirty-two minutes later and the interphone rings. I buzz him in and when I open the door to my flat, he steps back ever so slightly. It's almost imperceptible. I know I'm not looking my best. My skin tone is decidedly grey and the bags under my eyes look dreadful. He gets over it quickly enough and I invite him to come in and take a seat on my sofa. I make him a coffee (it's the done thing, after all) and as I do so he shouts through to me in the kitchen.

'As you've more than likely guessed, I'm here to see you about Stéphanie Tisserand. The woman we thought was missing?'

'*Thought?* Oh! You've found her, then!' I do my best to sound overjoyed at the news – cheered by such a successful outcome. I walk back into the lounge smiling. But . . . the major doesn't mirror my good cheer.

'Yes. We found her. But we found her dead, unfortunately.'

'Gosh . . .'

'We fished her body out of the Seine just near the Île-Saint-Denis.'

I need to find something to say here. I manage an 'I'm sorry', but it doesn't sound right to me.

I don't think he hears me anyway, because he carries on without acknowledging my words. 'Stéphanie Tisserand drowned.'

Of course, I'm dying to ask him whether or not it was an accident, but I know I have to hold back. He answers my question without it having been asked.

'We know she drowned. The autopsy has confirmed as much, but what we don't yet know is whether it was accidental or foul play.' It's at this point that he picks up his espresso from the table and downs it in one. 'Hmm. That's very good! Do you have an Italian cafetière?'

I confirm that I do, and he seems to rejoice in the fact.

He continues. 'Obviously it's our job to find out what went wrong, and I won't bore you with all the details. The only reason I'm here is that I just wanted to clarify a few points. May I?'

'Yes! I mean, that's why you're here . . .'

'Very well, then. So, are you still in possession of the hire car we talked about last time?'

Careful now, Régis. Prudence. 'Yes. I'm keeping hold of it for the moment . . .'

'That's what I thought.'

He clearly knows I haven't taken it back to Hertz. But why is he still interested in it? 'Does it have something to do with your investigation?'

'Not really. Not now that we know a little more about what happened. But to be honest, before we found the body, I spent a lot of time down in Auteuil and I didn't once see you or your Twingo. Have you changed where you like to go for your walks?'

What a question. I know that I have to be on the ball here and that it's time to play the cancer card. 'I wish that was it. But . . .' I'm ready to get the violins out. 'I'm going through a particularly difficult period in terms of my treatment. I'm sure you must have noticed that I'm not at all well.'

His cheeks flush with embarrassment and he makes an awkward attempt to contradict me, but he knows he can't possibly come across as credible.

'I understand,' he stammers.

'And so . . . my walks have been reduced to a short circuit across the road in the Jardin du Luxembourg.'

'I'm so sorry.'

And just to make him that little bit more ill at ease, I allow a loaded silence to fill the room before eventually breaking it. 'Is that why you wanted to see me?'

'Yes. But not only that.'

From the way he replies, I know I've achieved my aim. He's feeling out of his depth and I can tell the interrogation won't be going on for much longer. So he asks his last question – the one I've seen coming.

'I wanted to know whether or not you ever go down to Neuilly-sur-Seine . . .'

He might well be feeling awkward. I know that much, but what I also know is that I'm not off the hook. Maybe for today. But I'm not safe. What he took to be a simple coincidence is now fast turning into actual suspicion. Was my car spotted following her, or was it perhaps the waiting staff at the brasserie who have let on that I was hanging around for days and acting oddly? I don't know what's going on. I can't, can I? So I'll just have to be evasive in my response.

'I go down there on occasion, yes. I've been to meetings there. A lot goes on nearby at La Défense. Back when I was working full-time, I found a nice little cafe-bistro type place. It's on Avenue Charles-de-Gaulle, so I still go there now and again. And back when I was in better shape, I would sometimes go for a run along the Seine. There you go. But . . .'

'Uh-huh?'

I force a smile. 'I'm a bit surprised that you're asking me all these questions about where I go and what I do. Am I to conclude that I'm under suspicion for something?'

'Not at all. What on earth makes you think that?'

This doesn't ring true at all. He does think I've been up to something, but it's too early in the game for him to let on. I have to keep up with the questions.

'So why am I being asked all this?'

His reassuring expression is far from believable as he sits there inventing an explanation. 'Let me clarify and you'll soon understand. I found you because of the car. That's all. The registration plate details were in our files, so I ended up at the Hertz agency in Montparnasse and they gave me your contact details.'

'Yes, I know all that.'

'The software we use gives us all the information of the owner of a vehicle. A lot more than you'd think. It tells us straight away if there have been any infractions or parking tickets, etcetera. And the new parking meters are quite advanced now, too. Do you know the ones I mean? The ones where you have to put your bank card in?'

I'm getting a tight feeling in my throat. My brain is whizzing at the speed of light as I try to think back to whether I've ever used one of those machines. I know that the one on Avenue Charles-de-Gaulle wasn't like that. I always used coins for that. But what did I do with the one in the Bois de Boulogne by the river? How did I pay for my parking on the day I assassinated Stéphanie Tisserand? I can't remember!

'So, we know that you parked not far from where we presume the drama took place and probably at about the right time. It's come from the machine.'

'Oh,' I say, as if I couldn't care two hoots. 'You know where it all happened, then?'

'We're not sure, but we know that she regularly went for a run on the Île de Puteaux, and that's very nearby. And she was wearing running gear when we found the corpse.'

Why is he saying 'corpse'? Who says that? Why can't he just say 'body' like everyone else? It sounds nowhere near as sinister. And seeing as he's sitting in front of someone who's on his way out, it might be nice if he'd choose his words a little better. Don't they teach them these things at police school? Oh, I don't care. There's so much going on. They have so many bits of information to sort out. There's no way I can be the main suspect. I thought I'd been clever. That's the problem here. I think I'm so bright with my super IQ and academic qualifications. But I'm not. I put my blasted bank card in a parking meter. I'm no better than a common criminal. I'm going to have trouble getting out of this. It might not even be possible. I've got to try, at least. I might be able to buy myself some time.

'Remind me what date we're talking about here,' I try.

'It was the twenty-first of June.'

'Maybe . . . yes . . . I think I remember being in La Défense that week at the Grande Arche. There was a video game exhibition there. I used to play a heck of a lot as a youngster and I thought it might be good fun to go and take a look at some of the older consoles. And I remember going down to have a bite to eat at that place I told you about. The cafe place. But I went there on foot. And I left my car somewhere around there. Parking is a nightmare. But I can't guarantee it was on the date you're talking about. I have online banking, though. I can check what I spent on that day and where I was.'

I'm already on my feet and heading to my office to check my account details. I need to show willing here.

He stops me, though. 'Don't worry. If the head of the investigation or the judge deems it necessary for you to prove your whereabouts, it is within our power to do what's required. Your accounts will be checked. In the meantime . . .'

He stands to shake my hand. He wants to put my mind at ease with his words and gestures, but I'm not fooled. I know I'm suspect number one here, and all he's doing is waiting for me to slip up.

He confirms my fears with his final query. 'You've not planned to go anywhere over the next few days, have you?'

Chloé has already booked our tickets to Ibiza. Does he know? 'Not really. I have a friend who wants me to go away with her on a mini-break, but to be honest I don't think I'm really up to travelling at the moment. Not right now. But if I change my mind, is that going to be an issue?'

'I wouldn't imagine so. But if you do decide to go, I'd be ever so grateful if you could give me a quick call to let me know when you're leaving and when you expect to come back. It's just that I'll need to know what to say to my superiors if they do want to look into this any further. Do you still have my number?'

'Yes, I have your card.'

'I won't stay here bothering you any further, then. I'll let you get on. You take the time you need to look after yourself. That's the most important thing.'

I show him out. As we're walking to the door, I have an odd thought. I think of how much I will miss my flat if I wind up in the nick. Banged up. Inside. Or whatever the cool thing is to say these days.

Chapter 23

The Air Iberia A320 is waiting its turn at the end of the runway at Charles de Gaulle. It's a very busy time of year and the captain announces that we're sixteenth in line for take-off. We've been taxiing for twenty minutes already. How much longer is this going to take? Another half an hour? Another thirty minutes of sitting terrified in my seat, my nails digging into my palms with Chloé sitting beside me doing her best to keep me calm? The flight attendants must have made up their minds a while ago that I'm some sort of country bumpkin who's never left the farm.

The atmosphere on board isn't doing much in the way of helping my already shattered nerves either. It's the holidays. Everyone is talking too loudly and getting into the party mood. Most of the passengers are half-soaked on airport booze. Others have their headphones plugged into their mobiles or tablets and are doing their best to ignore the security demonstrations. And the flight is an hour and a half. This is going to be a long trip.

I called Major Charvin from the departure lounge just before the final call. I pretended that my friend had decided to surprise me at the last minute, and hadn't wanted to give me the chance to resist. He spoke to me very formally, telling me to enjoy my time abroad, as the judge had not deemed it necessary to look into me any further for the moment. He was very civil and matter-of-fact about it, and even stated that he hoped I'd make a full recovery. I thought about asking him how the investigation was progressing, but I decided against it. I know he is absolutely convinced of my involvement in the death of Stéphanie Tisserand, and so I'd be better off showing no interest in the whole affair. There'll be time enough for that later – because I haven't heard the last of him.

It's our turn now. We're lined up. The engines start to make a lot of noise. Too much noise. I press myself into the back of my seat as hard as I can and Chloé strokes my hand, which is now gripping the armrest. The skin has whitened with the effort. The passenger on my left is a young Spanish boy travelling on his own with a label around his neck. He is giggling at the sight of me in my panicked state. What an annoying little brat he is.

I don't come back into the real world until my feet have touched ground on the other side. I'm still dazed, though. I pick up the wrong bag from the conveyor belt. My brain must have just disconnected from reality during the flight. I don't even remember the landing. It's all quite fortunate, really.

'I think that's mine.'

I look down and see a young woman in her early twenties. She's staring at me crossly. I've no doubt as to her motivation for visiting the island. Her low-cut top reveals everything she has and it's clear she's here for a good time. A hen party or something, probably. I stare back at her for a few seconds as her words sink in. She's right. The bag I'm holding has a big sticker on it that reads: 'I'm famous.' And I'm not. So I hand it back to her, muttering an apology.

'Have a good one!' she says before flouncing off to join her friends, who are all laughing. *Have a good one?* It's phrases like this that I just never use. I know she's telling me to enjoy my stay, but the way people speak to one another now has really changed since my day.

Over on the other side of the conveyor belt, I can see Chloé is also amused. She points to my bag as it comes around. I pick it up and we leave the airport. The sun hits us hard on the way out of the doors. It's quite the welcome.

We take a taxi to the hotel, which she explains she booked at the last minute. Chloé does her best to cheer me up with her zest and enthusiasm – but to no effect. It's not just this trip and all the partying that's bound to be going on until all hours that's filling me with dread. I know that this is going to be a hotel from hell, full of incredible loud-mouths of limited intelligence screaming into the night. But if I force myself, I might even be able to join in the revelries. And it's not the highly anticipated killing of Nkomo that's bothering me either. I'm not really feeling the emotional impact of that at all. If I'm honest, it doesn't affect me one way or the other.

What I'm worried about is the major. It's like the sword of Damocles is hanging over me and I just can't relax. What's exasperating about it is that Chloé doesn't know a thing. And that's for the best. I think that's what I fear the most – her finding out about it. How will she react when she discovers how little care I took? And that I've attracted the attention of the investigating officers? Oh, well. It doesn't really matter. She's bound to find out at some point . . . but it'll be at a point when there'll be little I can do about it anyway. That's the real problem, I think. I'm actually scared. I have a cold and insidious feeling of dread. I'm afraid of dying unhappy. Alone. In a bare hospital room. I'm not feeling very brave at all. Should I just consider this another phase in my insipid little life? But that's no longer how I feel. I want to give it my all now. I want a final crack at living. I didn't think I was like other people . . . but I am. I'm having so many contradictory feelings these days.

It's worse than that, though. I find myself having inner debates at the strangest of times. I tell myself that I've spent forty-four years complaining about my life, moaning about having to live side by side with people who disgust me and belittling their selfish ways and mediocrity. I sometimes hope that all the catastrophes that climatologists have warned us of will happen sooner rather than later and that I'll be sorry not to see it. Then, on other occasions, I realise that I'm now at the point where I'm about to leave them all and instead of rejoicing as I should I daydream about it all being some big mistake. That it's just a nightmare. This constant battle is exhausting.

Our taxi driver is getting on a little. Every thirty seconds or so he moves his cigarette from one corner of his mouth to the other, pulls it out again and then spits out of the window. It's fascinating. We stop outside what I assume is our hotel. It's a humongous white building standing eight storeys high with a balcony at every window. A shiver runs down my spine as I read the sign above the door. Hard Rock Hotel. I'm terrified.

We're basically staying in a nightclub. *Good choice, Chloé.* She couldn't have ruined my last few days of existence any more if she'd tried. She notes how taken aback I look. In fact, my initial reflex is to just refuse to move from the taxi and make a getaway straight back to the airport. She has an apologetic look about her as she smiles weakly and assures me that, despite the name, it really is just a hotel and that it was the only room she could get us at such short notice in the same resort as Abdou. She also adds that, given the price, I should just desist with my grumbling.

Once we're inside, I have to admit that the place does seem fairly upmarket. There's a stunning pool in the centre of the building surrounded by floor-to-ceiling windows and with views over the gardens behind. If I wanted to parade around in my swimming trunks, this might be a great spot to do it. Plus, the whole place is virtually deserted. There can't be any more than three or four swimmers in there this afternoon. But does that mean that the hotel sleeps during the day and comes to life at night? I bet it does. To the left of the reception desk I can see a huge ballroom with a massive stage and the biggest speakers I've ever seen. There's a technician tampering with them. Fingers crossed he can't get them working. Oh, I'm not going to sleep a wink tonight. I can feel it in my bones.

The bedroom itself is exactly what I expected when I walked into the place. There are top-of-the-range gadgets, a flat-screen, and lights above the bed that change colour. Yes – *the* bed. It's a quadruple king-size (just guessing) but we're going to be in very close proximity to one another. There's a happy thought indeed.

'I'll get undressed in the bathroom and we can put some pillows between us if you want.'

This woman can always read my mind. It's frightening.

Like a little old couple, we choose our sides of the bed and set about unpacking our cases. Straight after this, Chloé heads to the bathroom and comes out in a swimming costume with a towel draped loosely around her.

'Coming to the pool?'

She asks the question knowing in advance what the response will be. There's not a chance in hell I'd exhibit myself in front of her, let alone perfect strangers.

'Go ahead. I'll stay here with the remote.'

'Ha! You and your telly! I won't be long anyway. I just want a bit of an energy boost and I'll be right back. Then we can get straight down to talking business.'

She disappears out into the corridor and I climb into bed, fully clothed, and start flicking through the channels. I've also just spotted the mini-bar and know I have six cool beers to keep me company. I take four of them out. It almost feels like being back at home.

Chloé didn't lie to me. I haven't even managed to drink half a can and she's back. Her wet hair is stuck to her forehead. She is still dripping and crosses the room on tiptoe to the bathroom, leaving watermarks on the carpet in her wake. When she comes back out, she's dressed and looking a bit more with it. She sits down at the foot of the bed, leans forward and helps herself to a beer from the bedside table, before downing most of it in just a few gulps. I'm not going to tell her about the two others in the fridge.

We get straight down to work.

'How should we get things moving, then?' she starts.

Something has shifted this time. I wasn't in the driver's seat with Guy Brison; it was all sorted out beforehand. But it seems that I have the starring role with Abdou Nkomo and that Chloé is counting on me to have all the ideas. I think if she had even an inkling about the bother I'm in with the major or my extra-curricular activities on the train, she'd be a lot less enthused.

'We're going to take our time. We have to start by visiting his hotel, looking into what he does with his days and nights, and then decide on a place and get it done at the last minute.'

'*At the last minute?* What does that mean?'

'Just before our flight back. We're on an island here. There aren't many ways of getting off it and it'll be better if we're long gone when his people in France learn of his death.'

'But say the opportunity arose and we had a quick way of getting out of here, we could get straight down to it, couldn't we? Get it done more quickly.'

This surprises me. She's usually so careful. She prepares every last detail and has so far shown herself to be infinitely patient. I've never known her to be like this. I tell her as much and she looks embarrassed. I have to ask her to explain herself several times before she'll give me an answer.

'Well . . . I was just worried about how ill you are. I'm sorry . . . but it's like the clock's ticking. I thought we might have time for one last little adventure after this one. I'm sorry.'

'Don't count on it.' I know I sound harsh, and she looks upset. I wait for her to question my attitude, but she doesn't. I continue. 'Listen, you know how hard it is to get flights during the summer. Everything's full. So our only option is to wait for the one we've booked. And don't forget that in two days I have to inject myself and then I'll be in a sorry state for a while. Not long . . . but it does reduce how much time we have available to us. Also . . .'

I pause at this point for emphasis. I want her to really take in what I'm about to say and have no doubt as to my sincerity and determination.

'Nkomo will be the last person I kill. I'm tired. I'm going to die in a few weeks and I want some time to myself. I want to be alone and prepare for this in peace.'

I expect these words to carry a certain weight and to trigger in Chloé the sense of compassion that they rightly deserve. But no. I forgot that she's as stubborn as they come.

She grins and says, 'Can I just tell you who I've got in mind?'

'Thule, I imagine?'

'Thule?'

I'm shocked that I have to refresh her memory. 'Yeah! The kid-killer! The one your soldier friend bungled?'

'Oh, him! No, there's no point worrying about him. There were complications with his surgery and he's not going to make it. I'd give him a couple of days at most. It's someone else.'

'I won't be changing my mind.'

'Don't speak too soon.'

OK. So her confidence works as the perfect bait and I allow her the pleasure of giving me further details. 'Come on, then. Out with it – but it won't change a thing.'

'We'll soon see.'

She's good at the whole suspense thing. She licks her lips, ready to savour my surprise, and leaves me hanging a few moments longer. Finally she comes out with it.

'I was going to suggest we kill Lionel Boucher.'

Lionel Boucher? How does she know about him? How on earth did she manage to find him again and how does she know about his involvement with me? Because he messed me up for a long time. He made my life a misery, in fact. It was back in high school when I first got to know him. I was the new boy at the beginning of the year; my parents had only just moved to the area. He was the top dog in the class. Everyone liked him, and all the girls were madly in love with him. Obviously. You know the type. But that's not all he was. Almost as soon as I showed up, he decreed that I was an oddball, to be ignored by everyone. I was a gibbering wreck for months. Years, even. It was harassment and physical abuse on a different level. I wasn't allowed to communicate with anyone. Not a soul. Even chubby Alain Gazon with his permanent acne wasn't permitted to talk to me. I bet he was just pleased that he was no longer the main target.

It didn't stop after high school. We went to the same university. I had to continue to see the cretin in the student union and around the lecture halls. His aggression towards me knew no bounds. I had (somehow) managed to ask one of the girls who lived in my halls out for a coffee. And he took her off me when he found out. He didn't really want anything to do with her and dumped her the first chance he had. He just wanted to bring me down a peg or two when I wasn't even up a peg. He couldn't just let me have my first little date with a girl.

Maybe I would have forgotten about him if it had stopped there. But we had a few acquaintances in common and on the odd occasion would end up at the same gathering. He would delight in humiliating me in front of an audience, always pretending that it was just innocent fun, but his behaviour was destructive. It destroyed me.

The last time I saw him was ten years ago. My divorce was being finalised. My ex-wife and I decided on an amicable split – all straightforward enough. But she chose him as her solicitor, not knowing of my past with him, and he took me to the cleaners. As soon as he found out who she was divorcing, he went all out. It was as if the only idea he had in his head was to bury me. The house, my pension, compensation – he threw everything he could at me, even though my wife had asked for none of it. If she had allowed herself to be influenced by him or hadn't been financially well-off herself, I would have been out on the street, living in some bedsit somewhere.

'What became of him, then?' I ask, unable to help myself.

Chloé's absolutely delighted. She knows she's struck a raw nerve and perceives the interest I'm showing to be an instant victory. 'He's a real bastard. He's a defence lawyer now and helps protect politicians and big tax dodgers – often one and the same – from any lawsuits. And . . . just as a little aside . . . he's been married twice. The first wife killed herself and the second takes so many antidepressants and sleeping pills that she's little more than a zombie these days. It would be a real act of kindness to do him in.'

She cocks her head to one side, like a little girl asking you to pay for her sweeties.

But I'm not biting. 'You'll be able to sort it out on your own. And my soul will feel a little lighter for knowing it.'

She doesn't keep at it, but I know her, and she isn't done with me yet. She'll pick up where she left off sooner or later.

For the moment, though, she gets back to her excitement about our current task. 'So, this hotel, the Bora-Bora – do you know exactly where it is?

'It can't be far. I have a map.'

'Shall we go and take a look?'

I don't quite have the same level of energy as her, but I manage to pull myself up to a less horizontal position. 'Yeah. Let's go. Let's go and kill Nkomo. That'll make us feel better.'

'You're getting more and more sarcastic.'

'I've got you to thank for that.'

Chapter 24

The hotel our dear friend has chosen is pretty much what you'd expect for your typical visitor to this island. It's just like ours. It has a dominating white façade, a gigantic swimming pool and a dance floor with a DJ's decks up on a stage. You could swap the two signs above the doors and nobody would know. It's just a two-minute walk from our place. And just like the Hard Rock Hotel, the Bora-Bora is half-asleep, awaiting the nightmare of an evening that I'm sure is about to commence. It also has direct access to the beach, and there are a few people sitting outside by a bar under a big parasol, drinking cocktails and listening to the booming techno coming from a giant sound system that they've somehow managed to erect on the sand.

We walk over to this outdoor bar, and I immediately regret not having changed before coming out. Even though I'm wearing light trousers and a shirt, I stick out like a sore thumb among all the bikini-clad women and half-naked men. People will just assume I work at the hotel, I suppose. This often happens to me – in the supermarket, in public administration buildings . . . I'm always being mistaken for a member of staff. I must just have that look about me; for some reason, I don't look like your average customer. And I don't look like the boss. I look like someone who can give you information. I really feel like turning on my heel and running out of there – at least until there are a few more people around and I'll be less noticeable. But I reason with myself, thinking that as Nkomo was always a real night-owl back in Paris, there's very little chance of him being out and about now, in the glaring sun. But you can hold back the applause for my excellent powers of deduction, because there he is lying on a beach towel just a couple of metres in front of us.

I am very quickly relieved to see that he's more than likely unable to take much notice of Chloé or me, given the state he's in. He is half-reclining, looking up lustily at a bronze-skinned girl in a tiny bikini. She's on a type of stand, a dance podium of sorts, and has something to do with the beach bar. She's there to advertise and is posing for him lasciviously. He has a brightly coloured drink in his hand and he's smoking a rolled-up cigarette which probably has something illegal in it. His head is bobbing up and down slightly to the music. He's off-beat, though, because he's clearly three sheets to the wind. I think back to what the barman at the Bronco said: *He's gone to ground.* I hardly think so. He's living it up. He is out of his mind and has no idea what's going on around him. He tries to put his glass down, but it slips out of his hand and spills all over his towel. He's not bothered, though. He puts his hand down his Bermuda shorts and starts touching himself. It must be a reflex action for him – but it has no effect. I'm sure even he doesn't think he's in a fit enough state to do what he wants to do.

Chloé and I exchange a look. She appears a little distressed, and I just fidget out of embarrassment. But we both know we're thinking the same things. The first is that we'd be doing humanity a favour if we get rid of this animal, and the second is that he's probably spending every day like this and that getting down to business won't be anywhere near as tricky as we thought. I might even end up changing my mind about what I said earlier. We could well be catching a flight home sooner than I reckoned.

Chloé goes to get us a couple of beers while I find a seat and continue to observe Nkomo. He has just stubbed his joint out in the sand and is now rooting around inside an Adidas backpack. I'm sure it's his personal pharmacy. From our lengthy observations of him, we've come to know his preferences in terms of recreational drugs. He likes to have a drink followed by a leisurely smoke, after which he tends to require a little pick-me-up. This means cocaine or an amphetamine. So I'm surprised when I see him pulling out a rubber band and a syringe. He must have had the wherewithal to source all this paraphernalia locally. He's not going to do this on the beach, is he? I know that they're fairly tolerant in terms of drug use on the island, but shooting up in public has to be a no-no.

The girl he's been looking at jumps down from her makeshift podium and rushes to him. She grabs everything with astonishing authority and shoves in back into his bag. At the same time, she is clearly giving him a piece of her mind – and not in the friendliest of ways. There's too much background noise for me to pick up what she's shouting. What's obvious is that her words aren't having much of an effect on Nkomo, who simply shrugs his shoulders. He makes a move to get the equipment out again, but in what must be a moment of lucidity he thinks twice and takes a look around him. I'm not in the slightest bit worried, because I'm too far to his right. He'll never turn his head around to that angle.

It looks as though he's thinking. He suddenly takes on an air of disgust, spits into the sand and scrambles to his feet. It takes a lot of effort. He manages to pick his towel up and throw it over his shoulder before moving away from the bar, further down the beach and away from us.

He is unsteady on his feet as he makes his way slowly towards another set-up on the sand. It's not a bar this time, but a boat-hire place with pedalos and kayaks. Chloé suddenly appears at my side and sticks a cold beer in my hand. I don't recognise the brand. I hesitate for a few seconds before handing it back to her.

'I'll just be a jiffy. Keep an eye on that dancing girl while I'm gone.'

I don't turn back to look at her, but I just know that she's standing there, watching open-mouthed as I follow Nkomo without taking even the slightest precaution. He's just a few metres ahead of me. His fat buttocks are wobbling as he tries to stay on his feet. He really is quite grotesque. His ankles can barely hold his weight and he teeters with every heavy step. He looks like a down-and-out. A nobody. If the men who work for him back in France could only see him in this state, I'm sure he'd lose a lot of kudos.

As he arrives at the boat-hire stand he looks around, not quite sure what to do with himself. He stumbles over to a small fence they've erected around the pedalos, sits down and leans against it. But it must be too uncomfortable for him and he stands back up. He then looks over to a rack where at least ten kayaks are stacked on top of each other. He must be hoping for a bit of shade next to that. But no. He walks over and decides against it. There's no cover there. I watch him floundering around the place and I note that I'm not in the slightest bit anxious, because he wouldn't suspect anyone was observing him. Not even for a second. It doesn't matter how close to him I get. I'm near enough to notice the spark of understanding in his eyes when he realises that he can hide behind the hut. There's room and shade enough for him there. I wait for a few minutes before joining him.

There is an old wooden rowing boat behind the boat shack, lying in the shade of a bamboo windbreak. He sits down in it, looking pretty pleased with himself. I'm surprised it can bear his weight. He looks like a beached whale as he quickly becomes absorbed in preparing his shoot. He doesn't even notice me staring at him . . . and I'm now directly within his sights. I decide it's going to be too risky from this angle and walk around the boat-hire shack to the other side. I'm now standing just a couple of metres behind him.

I watch the ceremony. He is heating the heroin on a little spoon with his lighter. He'll soon be filling his syringe. I've seen this in films. Once he's tied the rubber band around his arm, he'll inject, but it's a fiddly affair for someone so out of it. I know that with this kind of drug there are a few seconds of intense pleasure where the person is completely and utterly defenceless.

I struggle to think what to do next. But not for long. I spot his towel on the ground – he must have dropped it before heaving himself into the boat. I step forward quietly, crouch down and pull it towards me. Almost on autopilot now, I roll it lengthways, so I have a scarf of sorts.

I don't take my eyes off him the whole time.

I'm not surprised to see that it's an effort for Nkomo. His movements are laboured and although he manages to load the syringe he fails twice to tie the rubber band around his arm. When he finally succeeds, he pushes the needle into a bulging vein. As he presses down lightly on the plunger, I see a drop of blood appear on his arm. I creep forward a little more, still keeping a couple of arms' lengths between us. He still hasn't seen me . . . yet.

But in a mixture of pain and pleasure as the poison starts to take effect, his head rolls back and that's when his eyes meet mine. He looks surprised for just an instant and then this look turns to one of fury. I think that's the only reaction he's capable of. I wonder if he knows what's coming as I jump forward and with all my might press the rolled-up towel over his mouth and nose, pull him backwards and hold his head down on the bottom of the boat. He tries to fight back – of course he does, it's in his nature – but to little effect, for the drug has weakened him considerably. He has next to no upper body strength, but his legs are banging and thrashing around. I push the towel harder into his face and his eyes bulge out a little. I close my eyes and count to thirty in my head. I open them again and remove the towel. No reaction. He is perfectly immobile. I know I don't even need to check for a pulse. I shift myself along the side of the boat, so I can face him fully and observe him at leisure. I am strangely calm. No doubt I'm getting used to seeing dead bodies now. Just as I expected, there are no marks from the towel on his dark skin. Only an autopsy would detect the true cause of death.

I don't rush as I take a pack of tissues from my pocket and use one to pick up the needle that has dropped between his thighs. I am careful not to leave prints, using more tissues to cover my fingers as I examine the contents of his pockets and bag. As well as a small bar of cannabis resin, I find two more doses of powder and a bottle of Evian. I mix the powder in a little water. I don't bother with the heating part because I wouldn't have a clue, and I inject it into his left arm. I then put the needle in his right hand and brush at his clothes and body with the tissues, just in case I've accidentally touched him somewhere. I take one last look before I walk away. His body arouses no emotion from me still.

When I return to her, Chloé has moved to a little wicker sofa and is sipping her beer. She looks relieved to see me and moves to one side to make room. I sit down next to her and she hands me back my beer.

'Where did the girl go?'

'Some hot guy turned up and she went off with him. It was more or less straight after you'd gone. She looked very pleased to see him. They chatted for a while and looked to be walking back to the hotel and I haven't seen her since.'

'OK. So we can suppose that she's not bothered about Nkomo's well-being, then.'

'I think we can.'

The beer is awful. I put it down on the ground and stand up.

'What are we doing now?' she asks me.

'Nothing. Isn't that what holidays are all about?'

CHAPTER 25

Of course, Chloé wants to make sure everything has been done by the book. She walks along the edge of the water and glances over to the boat hut. We can just see behind it from this safe distance. She notices that, to anyone walking by, Nkomo could pass for some party-goer who's nursing his hangover and just having a quiet laze in the shade. She doesn't think that anyone would be unduly worried, if they were even to notice him. But she insists that we stay near the hotel until the body is discovered. It's nine o'clock in the evening before we finally see an ambulance show up and come to a halt on the small road behind the boat-hire place. And then nothing. It doesn't even make the local papers. Over the next few days, we don't notice so much as a police car anywhere near the Bora-Bora.

Chloé even dares to return to the spot on the beach where I left him. I don't have the guts to go anywhere near it. She notices absolutely nothing. The old boat is still in situ. There's no police tape around it to stop people approaching – no trace of an actual police investigation at all. The body has simply been taken away. That's it.

We start to wonder what the hell might be going on. The next evening, we decide to go for a fancy meal a little way from the town centre and the rabble there. We start a conversation in our schoolboy (or schoolgirl, in Chloé's case) Spanish with an elderly couple who were born and bred on the island. They tell us that they ran a hotel for many years, but had to sell the place when Ibiza stopped being the charming little seaside resort it once was and became a giant disco. They went to live in mainland Spain and only come back a couple of days a year now to see the few friends with whom they've remained in touch.

We admit that we don't feel particularly at ease here. They both laugh and say how they understand our attitude, and that we don't look like the sort of people to feel the allure of today's Ibiza. And this is where Chloé astounds me. She takes advantage of what they've just said to complain about the tourists and the state some of them seem to get themselves into, and says she's surprised that there aren't more serious incidents on the island. Our neighbours oblige her and affirm that there are indeed many incidents but that the police, encouraged by the local authorities, don't tend to look too closely, and just let most of them pass under the radar. It means the image of Ibiza can remain intact as a party destination, but a safe one. This allows us to leave the restaurant with the feeling that we'll never hear of Abdou Nkomo again.

We put the wheels in motion to get ourselves back to France in double-quick time. Me because I can't stand the decibel level of the place, nor the constant displays of extravagance on the part of the other hotel guests, and Chloé because even though I've repeated my categorical 'no' several times, she's hoping she can get me to change my mind about Lionel Boucher once we're back home.

As we imagined, we're unable to find an earlier flight; we're just going to have to make the most of things and enjoy the days that separate us from France as best we can.

Chloé spends a lot of time down at the pool, either in one of the many water aerobics classes she's signed up for, or sunbathing. She sometimes even goes to watch one of the shows put on by the hotel staff.

For me . . . it's a little more difficult. I had my injection over twenty-four hours ago and I had to stay holed up in my room until I was feeling ready to face the world again; since then I've taken the odd stroll, looking for calm spots away from the other holidaymakers to find a little serenity.

I find a perfect little place: a narrow creek with steep cliffs rising on either side. There's no way I can swim in it – it's far too dangerous – but it's a nice enough place to relax. It's a four- or five-kilometre walk from the hotel and I enjoy the exercise. I actually manage it twice a day – both morning and early evening, when the first bass notes from the dance floor start to shake the hotel walls.

I spend many hours there, lost in my thoughts; often dark thoughts. I watch the sea and do my best to enjoy its peacefulness. I try to convince myself that my calm and truly beautiful surroundings away from all the noise and bother of my fellow human beings is a taster of what is to come when I've passed over to the other side. But I can't see the merest grain of truth in it at all.

Yes, I hate the world I live in. Mankind repulses me to such an extent that, at the very end of my existence as part of it, I have been driven to kill several of its members in cold blood. You'd think that having reached this level of disdain for humanity I should be ecstatic to be getting out of here – to know it's over.

I think of the people who have pushed me into being so contemptuous. My parents, first of all. They loved me, but they loved me badly. And they left without completing their role. Then there was my ex-wife. I shared three years of reciprocal indifference with her, but she was the only one to know that, behind the bad-tempered façade on display most of the time, there is a good soul who might show his face on occasion. And of course there were others with whom I crossed paths. Those I didn't speak to, but with whom I exchanged a glance, or just a moment. Finally there were colleagues with whom I shared similar hopes, generous gestures or simply the occasional spark of goodwill.

I sometimes cry – something that hasn't happened to me since I was seven or eight years old; heavy tears drip down my cheeks without warning, and I have trouble understanding them.

It's two days until our flight. It's evening now, and I am sitting in my special spot having one of my existential crises when I see Chloé walking towards me. The sun is disappearing behind the pine trees on top of the rocks and I can only see her silhouette, but I recognise her gait.

She has the decency not to ask me what's wrong. Nor does she offer to console me when she plainly sees my tear-stained face. She simply sits down next to me and tucks her light skirt in under her thighs. She looks in the same direction as me – to the horizon, beyond the ocean. For me, it symbolises the lack of a future. A deadline.

The tears come again. She puts her hand gently on mine and asks if I want to go back with her. I shrug my shoulders, trying to communicate that it doesn't really matter where I am. I feel devoid of energy.

'I have a surprise for you,' she whispers.

A surprise. I know all about her surprises. She'll have found someone to kill or it'll be something to do with someone we've already killed. It'll be about killing, anyway. But I just don't have the strength to object and without asking for an explanation I get to my feet and walk back to the hotel with her.

On the way, I find her attempts to cheer me up a little on the ridiculous side, but they're not completely without effect. She allows me to think back on some of the more pleasant moments of my existence and as we enter the main foyer of the Hard Rock Hotel, I do feel in lighter spirits.

I imagine we're on the way to the bar, because we've been hanging out there rather a lot over the last week, but she guides me to the lifts and up to our room. I'm wondering whether the surprise she has in store might be one that we enjoy naked, but even having fantasised about it for so long, I don't actually think I feel like it, or am up to it. As things stand right now, I just want it to be two days later and to be back on home turf. And then I just want to wait it out.

I don't even have time to protest before she's opened the door and I see my surprise straight away. As promised. This surprise of hers takes my breath away and I can think of nothing to say for several seconds.

He is sitting comfortably on one of the armchairs, sipping a fruit juice. I hover, not knowing what to do next, and then step into the room. My thunderstruck look seems to have greatly amused him. He stands and, just as he always does in his office back home, invites me to take a seat. He returns to his own chair and Chloé squats down on the floor next to him.

'What does this mean?' I finally manage to splutter.

'It's nothing alarming. Quite the contrary, I assure you,' replies Professor Lazreg, his smile widening further.

He looks down at Chloé. 'He hasn't changed his mind about Lionel Boucher, then?'

'No,' she states matter-of-factly. 'Or if he has, it's a very recent decision.'

I don't understand a thing here. I can do nothing but look at one, and then the other, over and over again. I think I'm in shock. My thoughts are all over the place and I'm incapable of slowing them down. They know each other. That much is clear. But it strikes me that they know one another very well. They are partners of some kind. They look at me in complicit silence. This might well have been going on for years.

'Chloé is my daughter,' declares Lazreg after the lengthy pause, for he is the one used to giving people hard-hitting news.

'Your daughter?'

I am having trouble taking this in. There is not the slightest physical resemblance between the two – I would have noticed. Maybe in the eyes? Actually . . .

He must know what I'm thinking because he adds, 'We don't look much alike, I know . . . But that's quite normal. Chloé is my darling daughter. My only daughter. And my adopted daughter.'

They both seem to think this is all extraordinarily funny, but I don't.

Lazreg understands this almost immediately and hastens to explain. 'We've been waiting to find someone like you for a long time. Sincerely – even given the number of patients I see – I didn't ever think it would actually happen. But when you first walked into my office, you had that look about you; it's in the shoulders. And I knew you could do the job. Or jobs. When we talked, right back at the beginning, I sensed the loathing you have for people. And I imagined, rightly so, that you'd accept our offer. So I sent my daughter to you.'

'So it's you . . . who's had me kill . . . all these people?' I ask, finding it difficult to articulate. 'And you used your daughter.'

Chloé immediately comes to the defence of her father. 'No, it's not only him. We both wanted to get rid of them.'

'But I just don't get it.'

It's written all over Lazreg's face that he is still enjoying my disbelief immensely. He leans forward to answer my question with what looks like sheer delight. 'We can take each case one by one if you want. We already gave you reasons enough, but you'll soon come to understand a little more. Let's start with Arthur Reimbach.'

'There was the child rapist before him . . .'

'Grégoire Thule? That was just to lure you in. We knew that he didn't have long left anyway, and that someone close to one of the victims was going to deal with it. And, to be honest, on a personal level, neither of us really had anything against him.'

'Huh? But you gave me the name of that soldier you hired. Chloé, you told me he was an addict with HIV.'

'I made all that druggie-squaddie stuff up,' laughs Chloé. 'And you never thought to check out what I was saying, did you?'

Yes, I admit it: I had utter confidence in her every word. Infuriatingly, this just makes them laugh all the more.

'Right, just forget about that one,' I say with a sigh. 'Arthur Reimbach, then?'

'Monsieur Gaudin, listen. You must have clocked my ethnic origins and you've seen me decline many an alcoholic beverage. And you are fully aware of how much hatred that man bore towards people like me. I'm sure that his opinions disgusted you as much as they did most people. So . . .'

'Erm . . . Well, yes, that's true. But deciding to just . . . There are legal measures that can be taken nowadays, official institutions against discrimination . . .'

Lazreg raises his hand to stop me. Although he still wears a grin on his face, he looks at me fixedly. He lifts his hand further still, up to his temple, and starts massaging a small scar that I've noticed before but not given any particular attention.

'Do you remember the events of the first of May 1988?'

'The first? No. I imagine you're talking about some sort of protest? I was only fourteen at the time and all I was thinking about was algorithms and trigonometry. I'd even started my own theory on the speed of certain subatomic particles. So, no. Whatever happened on the first of May isn't something that's stayed with me.'

He barely takes any notice of my words and continues to explain. 'I was in my fifth year of medical school. I had two close friends in my class. Their families were originally from Tunisia, just like mine. We had the rather naive idea that we could just stand by the side of the road and watch as a group of neo-Nazis, who were masquerading as members of the Front National out on a march, stomped past us. We didn't even go down intentionally. We were on our way to a lecture. It was the first time the party had ever been out on a demonstration. The whole pretext was that they were celebrating Joan of Arc. Bad luck for us. We were beaten up. No, we were *savagely* beaten up. And for no reason whatsoever. Well . . . actually . . . "just for the hell of it", as I heard one of them shout in between kicks to my stomach. Two of us came out of it barely alive – but our friend never regained consciousness and has lived ever since in a vegetative state with his family in Tunis.'

'I didn't know that . . .'

'Of course you didn't! Nobody knew about it, because it wasn't made public.'

I wait a few seconds before saying, 'So, Arthur Reimbach . . . He was one of them.'

'The ringleader. I'd like to leave it there, if you don't mind, because I find the whole episode haunting and it's painful even to think of it.'

He does look sincere in his suffering. I understand his need for this act of vengeance – even if it was executed thirty years later. And Reimbach wasn't one of the good guys in my book, but still I'm left with a bitter taste in my mouth about not being told the whole truth . . .

For the moment, I'm trying to put events in chronological order. I feel so mixed up, though. I think of Stéphanie Tisserand. She came next, but what comes back to me is the night Chloé first presented me with the folder on my second victim.

'If I remember rightly,' I say, not really directing my words at one or the other as I feel quite indifferent as to who explains it to me, 'the two of you almost bumped into one another at my place. Was that done on purpose? Was something happening there?'

They laugh in tandem, but then Lazreg looks at Chloé in mock anger.

It is she who speaks. 'That was entirely my fault. I was overexcited about getting into this new little adventure of ours and I completely forgot that you'd be having your treatment. I took my chance when you went off to the kitchen to warn Daddy that I'd be there.'

'And then,' Lazreg continues, 'I tried to give you the impression that I was in a dreadful hurry, if you remember. I couldn't have you seeing me with my daughter and maybe putting two and two together.'

Yet again, they both look simultaneously amused and impressed with themselves. I don't share their hilarity at all. I have far too much on my mind.

'So, Stéphanie Tisserand,' continues Lazreg. 'She was just my ex-wife. It's as simple as that. We married in 1990 and I wouldn't say we had the happiest of unions. We didn't know it, but there were a lot of clouds on the horizon for us. Chloé, as I've said, was adopted. So you can imagine what some of those clouds were.'

'You couldn't have children?' I hazard.

'That's exactly right. And so much aggression built up between us. We explored several avenues – mostly medical, of course – but we finally turned to adoption and that's when Chloé entered our lives.'

They share a look. It is as if there's perfect harmony between them. This image turns my stomach a little. They love each other, but is it romantic love? Surely not. When they eventually take their eyes off each another, Lazreg turns back to me.

'Unfortunately, our happy little family didn't last long. My wife took a lover and fell pregnant just a few weeks later. She abandoned us and went to live with her new man and later gave birth to their son. People leave their husbands every day, but abandoning a daughter is something else entirely . . .'

I watch as Chloé's face transforms. The jubilation that has been plastered across her features ever since I came into the room changes into a grimace unlike any I've witnessed before.

'I was five when she left, and she didn't look back,' she says. 'I no longer existed as far as she was concerned. She refused to see me until I came across her, quite by accident, two years ago and made her hear me out.'

'After so many years of pain,' adds her father, 'it's a miracle Chloé is still with us. After that level of cruelty, how could we just sit back and do nothing?'

This means they used me to get back at her. I want to express how sickening I find it all. I want to scream. But the reality of what is happening here is too frightening. I can't take this in. I need time.

I also need further explanation. 'But I saw her with those two young girls. They were definitely working girls.'

'All set up,' confirms Chloé. 'I knew that you were starting to have doubts. We hired them. We also hired an actor who pretended to be a big potential client for her and her stupid agency. He sent her a car, a driver, a bodyguard and the works, and then, after their meeting at the Plaza, he asked my mother if it would be OK if they dropped off his "nieces". I would have loved to see her face at that precise moment.' She dares to add with a taunting tone, 'You were clueless, weren't you?'

I'm just appalled by her. She took advantage of my weaknesses, my naivety, my ignorance of the world and the people around me, my lack of discernment in certain situations . . . and most of all . . . my feelings. I see the faces of each of my victims like a series of flashes in my mind. Reimbach, Stéphanie Tisserand, the headmaster of that school, the guy on the train whose name I don't even know (but who I don't think I'll bother mentioning to Chloé and Lazreg) and Nkomo . . . my most recent victim. My arm muscles still ache slightly from pressing that towel so hard into his face. Were the other killings for revenge as well? This last one? I need to know.

'I imagine you've got more to tell me on the subject of Nkomo, then? What did he do? Are you going to tell me he wasn't even a dealer?'

'You know perfectly well that he was,' says Chloé. 'Don't get stroppy. But as you've guessed, that's not all he was.'

'Tell me.'

'He raped me last year,' she states in a perfectly neutral voice. 'I was in one of my depressive phases. I was mixing my medication with other drugs and alcohol. And I was out of it one night in this club and he made a beeline for me. He went too far. He took advantage and I swore I'd make him pay. It's done now, and I thank you for that.'

I give this revelation some thought. In fact, there's nothing very surprising about it. It corresponds perfectly to the man I killed earlier this week and had spent days watching. But now that she's mentioned the word 'rape', my mind takes me straight to the teacher. The paedophile, Guy Brison. He's the only one I don't know about yet and I have to ask.

Chloé's response sends a shiver across the surface of my skin. 'Brison was one of my primary school teachers . . .'

'Oh, I see . . . He . . . with you . . .'

Chloé scoffs. Her father joins her and they both seem delighted with what I've just said. They seem to be actually gloating over my gullibility . . . or stupidity. When they finally pull themselves together, Chloé continues. 'No! He never made sexual advances. Not towards me. Not towards any child. But you saw the man, didn't you? A jumped-up little headmaster, old-school style, with all his moral codes and virtues and all the rest of it. I mean, I have to admit that I was far from an easy child, but I became his whipping boy. Well, whipping girl. There were extra rules to follow for me, I had lines every lunchtime, a ruler across the knuckles at least twice a week. Pulling my hair was one of his favourites. The finer hair at the front – where it hurts the most.'

'What? That's it?' I manage to spit out, although barely audibly.

'What do you mean, "That's it"? You can't imagine what it was like for me. I had a terrible time of it, I can assure you. He had it coming. I can't tell you how good it felt when I saw you plunging that needle into his neck. It was pure joy – far better than I could have ever imagined.'

I'm going to have to get out of here. And sharpish. But, like she said, this isn't an island you can depart from just like that. Our flight for Paris leaves in twenty-four hours, and unless something else comes up I'm going to have to travel back with this woman who has managed to manipulate me as far as anyone can, I think. I trusted her so completely.

I am shaken to my bones. How could I have been so ridiculous? I need to get out and get some air. It's so very claustrophobic in here. I stand up, but it takes every scrap of energy I have. Lazreg flashes me a knowing grin, which makes me gag a little.

'Don't go. We have more to tell you.'

'It can wait, can't it? It's getting a bit too much for me.'

'No. This is important. It's about your treatment.'

'I know. You've prolonged my life so that I would do your bidding. I understand. Thanks, though.'

'No. That's not what I was going to say at all. Sit back down, please.'

I obey without knowing why, and he starts up again. 'When you first met my daughter, she told you that she had nothing to offer you in exchange for your services. That wasn't exactly true.'

'Is that so?'

'It is. We're going to reward you for all the hard work you've put into this. That's why I'm here. I didn't want to miss this part. I just couldn't wait. We're going to give you your life back.'

Chloé is starting to look very enthusiastic now and picks up where her father left off. 'You have to admit that your life was shit. Really shit! If it hadn't been, you would never have accepted our offer. So, here's your chance.'

She hands me a briefcase that's been resting at her father's feet. 'You have a choice. Either you continue on the course your life was taking . . .'

Lazreg opens up the briefcase to show me its contents. 'Or . . . you'll find a perfectly valid and authentic passport in here. If you want, you can become Cyril Burnet. You'll be Swiss. We've also put fifty thousand in there. Cash, of course. As well as the details of a bank account in Switzerland where you'll find another fifty grand. You can give me power of attorney to liquidate your assets in Paris and I'll send you through the corresponding funds – to the exact centime, and to that account.'

'But . . . you're forgetting my illness?'

'You mean your benign tumour? We got rid of that within the first few sessions of radiotherapy. But I needed to keep you in the dark about all that because, if you'd known, you wouldn't have been in the right frame of mind to complete our missions. I doctored your test results. But I can promise you this. Look me in the eye if you want . . . You have your whole life ahead of you.'

'What about all the injections?'

'Just a light emetic. Enough to make you feel sick for a few hours and make our whole story sound believable.'

'Come on! Just admit you're pleased about this and we'll move on!' the daughter has the gall to add.

CHAPTER 26

I've got my whole life ahead of me.

That's the first thought that enters my head upon waking, and I have to say that this prospect does fill me with an incredible sense of joy. A joy I haven't ever experienced before. I'm almost floating on air without a care in the world, and the best of it is there's no shadow of remorse bearing down on me. Even the faces of my victims that so haunted me last night are fading . . . becoming blurred.

I'm still a little dazed by everything they told me, but no more than that. As for the money they want to give me and the new identity – they can forget it. That sort of amount wouldn't really allow me to change my life that radically. And I don't want it anyway. I was so pleased to learn that my death has been put off, for a while at least – but simply because I want to get back to how it was before: I want to watch game shows, eat frozen pizzas and down 1664s, take up my work again with the team in Geneva and even get back into teaching . . .

Obviously, I'm going to need Major Charvin to get off my back for any of that to happen. Here's hoping he goes looking somewhere else for Stéphanie Tisserand's murderer, though I'm not sure I'm very optimistic on that account. But I can always ponder the matter when I get back to Paris, because for the moment, I still have these last few hours in Ibiza.

After a cold shower – let's call it lukewarm – I get dropped off at the port in a taxi. Despite all my fears about it being the middle of the season, I manage to find exactly what I'm looking for. The price is extortionate, which maybe explains why it remains an option, but I've never been much of a spender so I think I can allow myself this luxury just once. So, I am now in possession of a rental agreement for a small motor boat – ideal for a little trip around the island. Obviously, I've never travelled out to sea on my own and my experience as a sailor is limited to a couple of days on a yacht with colleagues, but there's a first time for everything and today is the first day of the rest of my life.

Before the big departure, I buy a few bits and pieces in town and go back to the hotel.

It's midday when the taxi drops me off. I find Chloé propping up the bar with her father. They are both stirring freshly squeezed orange juices as they watch me approach.

'Hi there, Régis,' says Chloé. 'How are things?'

'OK. Things are . . . starting to get better, I suppose. I've had a lot to mull over.'

'That's right. Now you've had a little time to think about it, how do you see things going forward?' asks Lazreg.

'Better. Things will be infinitely better. I can't hide the fact that I think your way of going about all this bordered on abusive, but on the other hand, the idea of this new life in Switzerland . . . It just . . . it sort of cancels all that out.'

'That's what you have to remember!' declares Chloé, sounding excited. 'I'm sure that our little escapade together will allow you to see life differently now. You're going to really make the most of the time you have left. Trust me.'

She's told me to trust her before and perhaps I shouldn't have. I feel like telling her as much. But it's pointless to go over it all again. I order a beer instead. It's a bit early for alcohol, but I suppose we all have something to celebrate.

The three of us clink our glasses together. 'Cheers!'

'No resentment, then?' asks Chloé.

'No resentment. But I do think the pair of you have rather inflated egos. If you don't mind me saying so.'

Lazreg lifts his glass again, as if to make a toast. 'Let's not get into that. I think you'll agree that our relationship now goes far beyond that of your typical doctor and patient.'

'Yes, I think I do agree with that.'

'Perfect! So I'll call you Régis from now on, if that's all right. I'd love it if you joined us for lunch, Régis, before we go our separate ways.'

'Oh . . . That's very kind of you, but . . .'

'Having lunch with someone else, are you?'

'No. Not at all. I've hired a boat. You know how much I hate crowds. I'm getting cabin fever on this island, and I need to get away for a few hours. You could both come with me, if you want? I'm sure we'll find a restaurant somewhere along the coastline. What do you say?'

'Why not?' replies Chloé. 'It might be nice! We should make the most of our last day together!'

I give them a few minutes to go and collect their belongings – swimsuits and towels – and then the three of us leave the hotel.

◆ ◆ ◆

After climbing aboard the boat, I start her up and we pull away from the port at a steady pace, leaving behind the busy beaches and dreadful din of the town. As I make a turn to the left to follow the coastline, I slow down. I have to keep my distance from the rocks and follow a route provided by the boat-hire company. We watch as more beaches come into view. Some of them have been taken over by those naturist people; it's all rather distasteful. But as we travel further around the island, the beaches become more and more deserted.

'I think that my favourite little spot is around here somewhere. I recognise the shape of the cliffs,' I announce.

'Do you want to stop here?' asks Chloé.

'I think it might be a nice idea. You guys could have a little swim, I'll look at the scenery and then we'll head off for lunch. The map says that if we carry on for a bit we'll reach the Torre de ses Portes and there are lots of restaurants on Las Salinas beach. What do you say?'

'You're the boss! Well, the captain!' she jokes.

There it is. My creek. My little hideaway. I slow down and make my way between the rocks. I have to avoid the sheer cliffs and stay in the central channel. Just a hundred yards or so and I can draw up to the pebbled beach. As we reach the shoreline, I turn off the engine and Chloé jumps down on to the stones below with her sandals in her hand. Her father is a lot less assured as he lowers himself down. He loses his balance and stumbles backwards into the water, just about managing not to fall over. His daughter grabs him by the elbow and pulls him on to dry land. I'm still on the boat. I bend down and reach for the heavy hammer, purchased just this morning, that I've hidden in an ice box.

I decide to go for Chloé first because she's by far the fitter of the two and more likely to put up a fight. From the height advantage I have on the boat, I'm able to lean over and hit her bang in the middle of her skull. I hear it crack. She's not coming back from that. She falls backwards into the shallow waters. Still hunched over from his near fall, Lazreg takes a couple of steps towards me and looks up with an expression of pure terror in his eyes. I strike another perfect blow. He collapses next to his daughter, half landing on her. It hardly makes a sound – just the faintest of splashes.

I jump down, pulling the ice box with me. I place it on the pebbly sand and continue to hit them. I hit and I hit without letting up. It feels like I'll never tire. Since meeting Chloé and discovering this second vocation of mine, never could I have imagined I'd use such a brutal, unrefined method. But I must say, it feels good. I didn't think they'd look quite so disfigured, though. If I continue at this pace . . . No, I can't . . . I'd better stop.

The water around them now runs red. But the blood starts to disperse, to wash away. Once we've gone, it'll only take a few minutes for it to return to a crystal blue.

I won't be putting the bodies back on board. I don't want to leave any traces. It would be too big a risk. I take out a chain and padlock from the ice box and tie them together by their feet. I then fix the boat's mooring cleat to Chloé's upper body. I push the boat a little deeper into the water, lift the ice box in and jump back in after it. The engine starts up on my first try. I've become a natural. All that's left for me to do is to drag the bodies far enough out to sea and to attach the heavy parasol stand that was also part of this morning's shopping list to the chains around their feet.

Epilogue

I'm sitting out on the terrace in front of the Bar du Caveau on Place Dauphine. It's now the end of September and the weather is still quite mild. Only the yellowing of the leaves suggests that autumn is upon us.

I'm going to order a beer – I can only hope that they serve 1664 in this place – and if I end up sitting here for a while, perhaps I'll allow myself to be tempted by a croque-monsieur with fries on the side.

I haven't brought anything to read. I don't even have my phone with me. With nothing else to distract me, I'm stuck with my thoughts.

I gave my first lesson in a long time this morning. When I walked into the lecture hall, my students all got to their feet and gave me a round of applause. It was embarrassing, but rather pleasant at the same time. I never thought I was held in particularly high regard. I also never thought I'd see any of them again.

I got back from Ibiza a couple of months ago now. I was so very scared that I'd have to resort to using that new identity I'd been given and disappear off to Switzerland, but it all went off exactly as I'd hoped.

Major Charvin showed his face again towards the end of August. Well, it was a telephone conversation, actually. He started off by asking after my health. I was on the defensive, but made sure he understood that I was in remission and hoped that it might continue a while yet. He sounded sincerely happy for me and almost forgot the real reason for his call. I had the fear . . . and was mentally preparing to pack a suitcase, order a train ticket to Geneva and a taxi to Gare de Lyon. But I managed not to overreact. I simply asked him why he was ringing.

He told me that he felt guilty at having worried a sick man unnecessarily and that, even though he really wasn't within his rights to tell me as much, he wanted to let me know what had happened with the Stéphanie Tisserand case. He explained that her ex-husband and adopted daughter, whose relationship with the victim seemed to have been beyond complicated, had both disappeared shortly after all the drama. The only clue they had was the father's car, which had been found in a car park at Charles de Gaulle airport. They believe that a quick getaway had been made and that the doctor was now the main suspect. Major Charvin said he was delighted to inform me that he wouldn't be bothering me again, and apologised for all the hassle.

I hung up and pictured the body of Professor Lazreg, forever entwined with that of his daughter, sinking . . . spinning . . . into the dark depths of the ocean. What with the warm water . . . and the crabs and other little sea creatures . . . I imagine there's not much of them left by now.

And so, I'm letting life get back to normal. But with a few added nuances.

I go out more. I'm interested in things that I wouldn't have bothered with before. I went to the cinema for the first time in ten years the other day. I also have the semblance of a social life now. My neighbours – the journalist and the former minister – actually invited me over for dinner one night. And that's where I met Marielle.

She's a project manager with the Red Cross. She adores going to the theatre. So we've been to see two plays. And they weren't half bad. She's also very much the sporty type. She took me down to the Jura Mountains and we went hiking for three days. I've even been to the gym with her. She wants me to join; she thinks it'll do me good. Perhaps I should listen to her.

A lot has changed. I don't even know what game shows are being broadcast at the moment. I can sleep without taking pills. And I don't always sleep alone. Really, my diet is the only thing that's stayed the same. How long will all this last?

Why have I made these changes? Is it because of what I went through with Chloé? Is it because I no longer have a death sentence hanging over me? Perhaps I shouldn't ask myself too many questions.

A new life. That reminds me . . . I was getting down to some paperwork the other day, opening up letters I'd left in a pile, and I came across the estimate sent to me by the funeral home I'd visited all those months ago. It was for my cremation and the transportation of my ashes down to Charentes. I wouldn't dare tell them the truth if they were to contact me again. They probably think I'm dead already.

I don't even have time to order my beer in the end, because there he is. Lionel Boucher. I recognise his frame as he walks steadily down the steps in front of the Palais de Justice. I know his pretty little two-seater Mercedes is in the underground car park across the road because I went down and checked earlier. I also took the time to smash the surveillance camera for that zone of the car park. I don't want to be disturbed by some jumped-up security man.

If I can't manage it today, I'll do it tomorrow. It'll take a while to fix that camera. And there'll be plenty of other occasions too. It's not like I don't have plenty of other work to be getting on with. I'm thinking about other people in my class. Others who were always up for humiliating me. Lionel wasn't the only one. Aurélie Lafarge was another. She should be fairly easy to find.

And then there's the boss of this very cafe I'm sitting in. I watched as he refused to serve a young man the other day because of his wheelchair taking up too much space on the terrace. I'll have to free up some time so I can get to know his route home, where he lives, what time he leaves and so on. You never know. The information might come in handy.

But there's no rush. Let's just take things one at a time. Method and organisation are and always will be the keys to success. I no longer have just six months to kill. For now, at least.

About the Author

Enzo Bartoli was born in the Bastille district of Paris long before the bearded hipsters moved in. He left school at a very young age and entered the world of work in a multicultural Paris which he would later use as inspiration for his novels.

His professional career saw him walk several paths – some of them surprising, to say the least. From a mechanic's workshop to a communications agency and the bar of an infamous dive, he finally became a journalist and rediscovered his love of reading. When he was done with the classics and had made his way through a substantial portion of the bestsellers, he decided it was perhaps time to give it a go himself, and has since written several novels set in the city streets and criminal underworld of Paris.

About the Translator

Back in 2001, after having read Philosophy and French at the University of Leeds and realising that being able to write a decent essay on Kant's Categorical Imperative didn't leave her with a great many career options, Alexandra Maldwyn-Davies decided to move to Paris, where she embarked on a career in writing and translation.

She is currently working on two projects of her own: her first novel and a sourcebook, *Women in Translation* (a collection of writings and articles on translation from the female perspective). She has steadily built a successful freelance French-to-English literary translation business and can now boast that she does what she loves every day of her life: she tells stories.

She lives in rural Finistère with her daughter (a future bilingual genius if ever she met one) and a motley crew of thirteen rescued dogs and cats.